AF264249

BELFAST
A TIME TO DIE

BRIAN WILSON

Disclaimer

This is a work of fiction based upon historical events. Other names, characters, organisations, places, events, and incidents are either the products of the author's imagination or used in a fictitious manner. Any resemblance to actual persons, living or dead, is purely coincidental.

ISBN (paperback) 978-0-473-69154-7
ISBN (hardback) 978-0-473-69155-4
ISBN (kindle) 978-0-473-69157-8
ISBN (Epub) 978-0-473-69156-1

Other books by Brian Wilson

SHORT STORIES

Moments in Time A collection of short stories, 2012

Bumpy Roads A collection of short stories, 2013

Here Comes the Sun-Perhaps? A collection of short stories, 2015

So that's Life? A collection of short stories, 2016

NOVELS

Operation Iran, 2016

The First Trumpet, 2017

Treasure of the General Grant, 2020

BOOKS FOR CHILDREN

The Night Before Christmas (parody) 2020

The Owl and The Pussy Cat (parody) 2020

The Guard is Changing at Buckingham Palace (parody) 2021

ACKNOWLEDGEMENTS

In writing this novel I have been encouraged by the ongoing support and feedback from my wife, family, friends and other readers.

I would also like to thank those readers who have taken time to write honest reviews of my book on the Internet. For a writer, such reviews are important and provide the necessary feedback and incentive to keep on writing.

My Facebook page is https://www.facebook.com/brianwilsonauthor

My Website: https://www.brian-d-wilson.com/

Chapter One
Belfast January 1977

"The best laid schemes o' Mice an' Men
Gang aft agley,
An' lea'e us nought but grief an' pain,
For promis'd joy!"
Robert Burns

There was an eerie presence that chilly January evening in 1977 as the two men and a teenage boy moved briskly down the dimly lit Belfast Street. The night was cold and still, the calm before the storm; the same stillness in the air and deathly silence that precedes a snow fall. But weather was the least of their worries as the three remained silently focused on their life-threatening mission that lay ahead. One of the men, Danny O'Malley, nursed a small well-worn, brown leather case, the contents of which would change their lives, and those of others, forever. Ahead, in the distance, glowed a warm welcoming light — a pub, one of the many along Shankill Road.

As they drew nearer, the deathly silence of that evening became broken by a chorus of pub-chatter and laughter. As this grew louder, Liam O'Mahony dropped behind allowing just Danny and his thirteen year old son, Sean, to proceed ahead towards the entrance. It was a popular, crowded pub overflowing out onto the pavement but even here the air had become stale with cigarette smoke. Through the choking mist and crowded interior, Danny and Sean inched their way towards the bar where Danny placed the case carefully onto the floor. Above the background of noisy chatter and laughter he managed to order a Guinness. While the barman was attending to his order, Danny surreptitiously checked his watch then clandestinely glanced to his left to confirm that the Shankill Butcher gang were seated as usual in their far corner of the room. There they were, a motley gathering of Ulster loyalist thugs seated around a wooden table, chatting and laughing and drowning in Guinness; a notorious gang who had been responsible for murdering, kidnapping and torturing many Catholics. Above their heads, hanging on the centuries old nicotine stained wall, hung a portrait of William of Orange conveying to the patrons that this was a Protestant pub. William, their hero, had deposed the Catholic James II as King of England in the Glorious Revolution of 1688. It was in the final battle, the Battle of the Boyne in Ireland, that William cemented his position as King of both England and Ireland. One thing's for sure, thought Danny, their hero wouldn't be hanging there for too much longer. Soon he'd be smashed to smithereens as he should have been when he dared to land at Brenham in the south west of England. Danny caught Sean's eye and gave him a nod to confirm all was going to plan. It had to be as everything had been meticulously rehearsed. Exact timing was critical, their lives depended upon it.

Danny and Sean's entry had not gone unnoticed despite the distraction of a young woman in a mini skirt, generously displaying her shapely legs. Nothing escaped the members of the Shankill Butchers sitting in the far corner of the room; they abruptly stopped their conversation and turned to suspiciously eye up the newcomers.

"Check them out," ordered a plastered Gerry Curry, who appeared to be in charge given the absence of their notorious leader Lenny Murphy.

"No need, he's no dosser, Gerry," replied Tommy Hegarty. "We know this one for sure; checked him out many times. Always the same results: stockings, stockings and more damn stockings."

He laughed together with some of the men then he continued. "A regular here; at least has been for the last few months. Tragic, his wife was killed in an IRA street bombing in Falls."

"Bloody murdering taig," roared Gerry Curry, clenching his fists and thumping them down on the table.

"His name's Danny," added Tommy. "Stockings salesman. All you find in his case are lots of women's stockings."

The men laughed again.

"Sounds a good job to me, something hard to find these days" chipped in Eddie O'Conor who seemed to be a little less inebriated but somewhat infatuated by the woman in the mini skirt.

"Any jobs hard to find these days," interjected Patrick Fitzgerald, a short stocky man of about forty, "and they give them to the bloody Catholics." He'd been unemployed now for over a year.

"That's if he gets to try them on the ladies' legs," continued Eddie. "I'd love to put some on that floosie over there. Now she's a fine thing."
The men laughed.

"Now, how do you get a job like that?" he continued.

The men glared at Eddie, who was now somewhat mortified and turning a slightly pinkish complexion.

"Well, they do need to try them on before they buy, don't they?"

The men continued to glare at him, then they all burst out laughing.

"Don't take it badly we're just codding ya," laughed Tommy.
The men all chuckled again.

"Now Eddie you're a married man," teased Gerry. "What would the misses say? Did you try on any of the stockings yourself, Tommy?"
The men all burst out laughing again.

"The stockings wouldn't fit these fat legs, Gerry," laughed Tommy, nicknamed 'Crusher' because of his sheer size. He had flattened and seriously injured many Catholics after using them as a trampoline.

"OK, guess there's no need but I won't object if any of you want to investigate." Gerry looked satisfied. "You may want to buy the misses a pair or try them on yourselves or even on that floosie over there, Eddie."
The men all laughed again.

"The man's harmless," replied John Coyle. "Seriously, he's hardly going to be standing there drinking piss, boyo at his side and a bomb ticking at his feet. Come-on, even Shane O'Doherty wouldn't do that."

"Good point," replied Gerry as he continued to observe Sean and Danny at the bar while the others returned to eyeing up the floosie and making rude remarks.

Danny was now standing at the bar with a Guinness in his hand and chatting to his son. "Keep an eye on my case, lad," Danny instructed his son loudly, so as to be overheard. He took a few more large gulps then put his glass down onto the bar and disappeared into the crowd.

"Now where's he off to?" enquired the barman. It wasn't often a patron walked away before downing the full contents of their glass of Guinness; at least not in Ireland.

"He'll surely return for his pint of Gat," lied Sean. "Off to post a parcel. That's where he's gone."

"Sorry, a parcel?" The barman looked perplexed and a little worried.

"He's off to the jacks," laughed Sean. "The man can't help himself. Half a glass of the black stuff and his bowels start to move."

"Oh, there's plenty of wrapping paper in that little room," gagged the barman and they both laughed. "Ha, ha, the job's not done until the paper work's finished. That's what they say." They laughed again.

"He's a gas man?" suggested the barman laughing.

"Is he ever," laughed Sean. "I could help by finishing that black stuff you know," offered Sean referring to the half empty glass on the bar. "It looks lonely just sitting there untouched on the bench."

"A good try but not here my lad, not in my bar. You know the rules. But when you're a few years older, then you can come here and drink to your heart's content and keep my till ringing," laughed the barman. "I won't at all mind taking your money."

"What's this?" growled Liam O'Mahony who had come from behind Sean and was now grabbing him by the collar. He turned towards the barman. "You know the law, you could lose your license, the boyo's underage and shouldn't be here. Come on out lad."

"Let me go!" cried Sean.

"He's with his dad," replied the barman. "Leave the poor lad alone. His Dad will be back in a few minutes."

"Still unlawful," replied Liam. "The lad can wait outside." With that he jerked Sean in the direction of the exit.

"But—my father's case! I promised him. Let me go! He'll be back soon." Sean screamed as Liam started to shunt him towards the exit.

"Out you go Boyo, the law's the law." Liam continued to push the boy through the crowd catching the attention of some of the concerned patrons.

"Leave the poor boyo alone," demanded one of the patrons but went no further as Liam was a well-built man who looked to be able to handle himself in a fight. Liam continued to shunt Sean towards the exit.

"I'll keep an eye on it," yelled the barman, referring to the case, so he could be heard above the pub chatter.

This too had not gone unnoticed by the Shankill Butchers and in particular stocky Shane Gallagher. This was his pub and he was not at all happy seeing the boy mishandled and shunted towards the exit by some cowardly bully who deserved to be flattened. Shane, nicknamed 'Knuckles', because he was handy with his fists, sprang up from his seat. He was a hot-headed redhead and Liam's actions had quickly driven him to rage. Nobody in their right mind should mess with this psychopath who had beaten many Catholics to a pulp. He and Basher (Bobby Bates)—one of Lenny Murphy's sergeants were two of the most dangerous men in the gang and in Belfast.

"How dare he?" he roared in a deep voice. "I've work to be done," he announced, clenching his fist into a tight ball and smashing it into the palm of the other. He left the table in an uncontrollable rage, shoving patrons out of his way while others in his pathway quickly dispersed rather than face the wrath of a madman on a mission.

"Go Knuckles," shouted Eddie. "Haha, another one beaten to the pulp. Now how many is it this week?" The men all laughed and remained seated, enjoying their Guinness and this entertainment. In the Shankill Gang there was never a dull moment. Knuckles was a war machine to behold and he needed no help. It would be an even more entertaining evening when he returned to give his account.

By the time Shane had reached the door the two men and boy had long since disappeared into the darkness of the night. It was only then that he realised this had all been staged and that now a case carrying a bomb was sitting unattended by the bar ready to explode and kill his mates. Shane in an uncontrollable rage swore and muscled his way back inside shouting

"Bomb—it's the bloody moron's case, get out!" before making sure that he wasn't held back from his own exit through the stampede that would surely follow.

But the stampede never eventuated; it was more a crushing of bodies that followed as the patrons pushed and shoved for dear life towards the bottle-neck of an exit. In this case they were more likely to die of asphyxiation, from the crushing and the choking cigarette smoke, than by being trampled underfoot or blown apart from an exploding bomb. Their escape was further impeded by those gathered outside, oblivious to the situation, and blocking the exit. Inside the pub, the Shankill Butcher Gang were seated in one of the worst places, having occupied one of the far corners. The skinnier members like Eddie O'Conor, could make their escape through a window but for others like big Tommy Hegarty there was no alternative but to join the push towards the exit. He used his muscle to callously throw aside those blocking his escape route as he made his way towards the exit.

Meanwhile, Danny, Sean and Liam were relieved to put some distance between themselves and the pub and to walk away unscathed.

"Let's celebrate, I could murder a Guinness or two before dinner," said a cheerful Danny, assuming they were now safe. This had been their most daring bombing to date and should deal the Shankill Gang a nasty blow.

"A pint of gat Da when you couldn't down your last?" Sean taunted. "You know what effect that has on your bowel." The men laughed.

"Best we go home but a pint of the black stuff would've been nice. It's going to get awfully nasty out here and I'm hungry." Liam's stomach started to rumble in agreement. "We're not yet out of the woods."

"That was the best ever," bragged Danny. "Everything worked exactly to plan."

"Hasn't yet," Liam reminded, as they looked back. "The bomb's yet to explode, if it does."

"What do you mean if it does? Oh! I can assure you that it will," said Danny. "Sean and I have never produced a dud yet, have we son?"

"That's right," added Sean. "This one's sure to bring the house down and the band hasn't even started playing."
They all laughed.

 As they were about to turn down another street where their car was parked, they paused to witness the explosion. It didn't take long for the eerie silence to be broken suddenly by a loud boom which shook the ground under their feet. The corner on Shankill Road erupted into a huge fireball.

"Now we just have to wait for the Garda," joked Danny.

"That's right," Sean said, laughing.

"No laughing matter. We'd better leg it before they arrive," urged Liam as they stood there still admiring their handy work.

The three ran down the road to where their car had been parked ready for a quick getaway. Literally minutes after the explosion, when the three were close to reaching their car, they heard the sirens.

"Holy Mother of God, it couldn't be, the bomb's just gone off. The Garda already?" A surprised Liam unlocked the car. "Come on, we're gone." They jumped into Liam's old Humber Hawk.

Liam had just pulled out the choke and started the engine when the sirens grew louder.

"Holy Mother of God, get down! They're coming our way!" Liam turned the car lights off and they all sunk down into their seats out of sight. They sat there with the motor idling, waiting for the cars to pass. One car passing slowly by, suddenly stopping in front of their vehicle while the other drew up behind.

"What the...!" Liam exclaimed. "We've been set up."

Four armed policemen approached the car.

"What's the problem?" asked Liam who had wound down the window and had placed a cigarette into his mouth to look relaxed and innocent.

"Did you have fun boys?" taunted one of the policemen, shining his torch into their faces.

"Out! Boys, you are under arrest."

Chapter Two

"All who draw the sword will die by the sword."
Matthew 26:52

Freezing in a cold concrete cell overnight that reeked of urine was not what Danny had planned. He looked across anxiously at his son Sean, now his cellmate, huddled and shivering in a corner covered in a blanket not much wider than his body. All he could manage was, "I'm sorry son, try and get some kip." How could he have done this to his own son?

Where was Liam? He'd been taken away in the second police car and was now presumably occupying another cell at the Royal Ulster Constabulary. Over that never-ending, unbearable night neither Danny nor Sean slept. Sean's occasional sobs reminded Danny that his son was still a child and this was no place for him. Even when they managed to drift into a doze they were quickly aroused by blood curdling screams coming from another part of the building. Hopefully this was one of the many drunks known to frequent these cells. The Irish did like their drink and, on occasion, even Danny had had to sober up in a cell. Danny had heard rumours that the authorities used torture to extract information from IRA prisoners. Maybe it was true and perhaps they could be torturing Liam. If so, then what was planned for them? Surely they wouldn't touch Sean. He was just a boy. "They won't get anything out of me," he mumbled.

The next day was just as unsettling until a policeman appeared with food. Both Sean and Danny's eyes lit up with hunger. Despite the food not being particularly nice they licked their plates clean.
When the policeman returned to collect the trays, Danny turned to him complaining, "I wouldn't even feed my dog that food."

"You're lucky that it wasn't poisoned," snarled the policeman. "If you thought this was bad, then wait until you see what they dish you up in the Maze."

The policeman looked over at Sean and sniggered. "As for your boyo, do you know what the men do to young lads in prison?"

"Over my dead body," replied Danny.

"And it will be, that's for sure." The policeman chuckled as he left both in a distressed state.

"Over my dead body," replied Danny

"And it will be, that's for sure." The policeman chuckled as he left both in a distressed state.

Other than the policeman, who relished the opportunity to mock them each time he came with food, no one else visited that day. Danny began to worry about his wife, daughter and elderly mother and their safety. They would have been concerned when he and Sean hadn't returned home. Danny suspected that surviving members of the Shankill gang would seek revenge even to the extent of hunting down family members. They were a vengeful, sadistic mob who would stop at nothing. Both Danny and Sean were disappointed they'd heard nothing about the bombing and how successful they'd been. Their isolation became even more unbearable with another cold night ahead to survive.

Danny turned to Sean who looked pale, scared and cold. "This is no place for you son. If they ask, you say that last night we'd been out visiting Grandma, right? And Liam kindly agreed to take us in his car as we can't afford one. We know nothing about the pub. Besides, you're a boyo and wouldn't be allowed in."

"What will Liam tell them?" murmured Sean, "since we're not together to corroborate our stories?"

"The same," replied Danny. "It was a backup plan in case we were caught and separated. I just can't understand how they were onto us and so soon. Everything was so perfectly planned."

"We were betrayed, Da. Somebody wanted us to take the fall."

"I think so, maybe a mole in the IRA," replied Danny. "It won't be the first time the British secret service has planted moles in the IRA."

Four days passed by and nothing had changed. Danny understood that laws had been passed allowing incarceration without trial for anybody suspected of being in the IRA. He thought that this law had been repealed but maybe it hadn't. So, were the authorities just going to leave them to rot in prison?

Or would they die of pneumonia or food poisoning first? Maybe they would just go mad from the isolation or having to persevere with the overpowering smell of urine. Didn't they have rights to a lawyer and how legal was their long detention? Danny was grappling with these thoughts when two policemen approached the cell. Not surprisingly, he was reluctantly separated from Sean and escorted to an interview room. Here he was firmly instructed to sit and remain seated. The policeman's belligerent demeanour suggested that he would be facing at least a grilling or even torture in order to confess.

Danny was left sitting alone in the small and dingy room, though much cleaner, warmer and better smelling than the cell. The shiny area on one wall, he presumed, was an observation window but he didn't care. They could watch for all they liked. He just didn't care anymore about anything. Danny rested his arms at full length across the table in front of him and rested his head. He felt exhausted from the lack of sleep and was not looking forward to being interrogated or worse, tortured. He just wanted to sleep and wake up with the realization that this was all a bad dream. It had to be as everything was so well planned. How could it have turned to custard?

"Oh dear, what are we going to do with you?"

Daniel, startled out of his stupor, looked up. An elderly policeman in his sixties had entered the room and had made his way to a seat directly across the table. He was immaculately dressed and groomed; his seniority and appearance suggesting he'd be more than a worthy adversary. Danny dragged himself up from the table and, mustering up what energy he had left, leaned back in his chair to convey defiance.

"We weren't wasted, so why are we here?" demanded Danny. "And where's Liam, the other man? I have my rights."

"You're in enough trouble already without worrying about your colleague. I think you know very well why you're arrested," the policeman shook his finger. "If we let you out now, then you're both as good as dead. There's already a price on your head so I hear. If we incarcerate you then you are likely to end up in the Maze with Gusty Spencer and some of his cut-throat Protestant gang who are doing time. How long do you think you'll survive? Oh dear, your prospects do look bleak. Whatever happens, you're as good as dead either way."

"You can only die once," replied Danny. "Anyhow, you're assuming I'm guilty of something. Visiting my elderly mother, the oul dear, is hardly a crime. Don't I get a lawyer?"

"Oh! Have you heard of Shane Gallagher whose nickname is 'Knuckles'?"

"Who?" asked Danny. "Shane who?"

"You know very well who I'm talking about. He's one of the people at the pub you bombed," said the policeman.

"What pub?" queried Danny. "There are pubs on every corner. As I said I was visiting Ma. I have to keep an eye on her, you know. She has Alzheimer's."

"Now, Gallagher's not at all a nice character," continued the policeman. "Has a lot of nasty homicidal friends. Most survived the bombing and he is not at all a happy chap. The rumour is he's out to get you after you killed and injured some of his mates. Now we've been trying to nail this thug for many years, for some assaults and murders. He'd willingly come here and identify you but the truth is we don't want our building torched. Then we have many other survivors including the barman, who says he could recognise you if required. Now he would make a very credible witness, though you may not now recognise him. The poor man received some nasty scars from broken glass during the explosion." The policeman looked over at Danny and shook his head. "What you did was really thick. Look, we knew all about the bombing— an informer from your own IRA. You were betrayed. Why do you think we were so quick to the scene?"

"I did wonder that myself. So where to now?" asked Danny. "My boyo, he's innocent. The cell's no place for a child."

"Not what I heard," replied the policeman. "He's just as guilty. You live by the sword then you die by the sword my lad. Many who were at the pub are swearing revenge and believe me some you'd not want to mess with. Meanwhile, I've suggested to your wife that she moves home for her own safety."

"Thank you," replied Danny. "I was worried about Deidre."

"Your actions may have been bold but they were totally stupid, especially for a WWII war hero," continued the policeman.

"Oh!" Danny looked surprised. "You've been doing some homework."

"You only needed one gang member to look in your case and you'd have been history," continued the policeman.

"Don't I know it," replied Danny. "We all would have but that was a risk worth taking."

The policeman shook his head. "And you went ahead and involved your son, a young boyo? What on earth were you thinking?"

"It was stupid," replied Danny, "but it had to be done. The gang had to be stopped from killing and injuring our people. My son was innocent though." A police officer entered the room with two cups of tea and Danny was handed one.

"So, you were in the air force during the war?"

"I joined in 1945 at age eighteen. We carried out bombing raids over Europe in Lancaster Bombers, bombing places like Dresden, Hamburg, Munich and Dortmund," replied Danny, who was more than happy to change the subject. These were memories of better times when he never felt like a second-class citizen.

"So the Lancaster, is that the one with guns in the front and back?" asked the policeman.

"And also the midsection." Danny had now perked up. The war had been an eventful part of his life and he had lost many companions as the life expectancy of Lancaster crews could be measured in hours rather than days. Most raids were at night which increased their life expectancy, even though the German searchlights were very effective and once in the spotlight the plane was a sitting target.

"So what were you, the pilot or gunner?" asked the policeman.

"The bomb aimer. I directed the bombs," smirked Danny. "I also operated the gun at the front," he added.

"Bomb aimer, that figures," the policeman grinned. "Bomb aimer, now there's an irony. Then you of all people should know how dangerous bombs are." The policeman took a sip of his tea. "And one never knows when a bomb might explode prematurely," he added. "I remember working on the case where two of your IRA colleagues were killed in Dungannon when their bomb unexpectedly went off."

"Always a risk," replied Danny, "but this gang had it coming. They've been murdering, kidnapping and torturing Catholics, and the Garda do nothing. Absolutely nothing. When the system is broken the people have to take the law into their own hands."

"That's not true," replied the policeman. "Along with the army, we have applied all sorts of measures to keep the peace. We've barricaded roads, run checkpoints, frisk searched for weapons and carried out surveillance and many other measures and you say we've done nothing! We administer the law which is applied irrespective of your religion and where we have evidence, then we will make arrests. Your case in comparison is straightforward. We have many witnesses who can identify you and your son. The fact is that you and your son will be locked away for donkey's years if you both survive the ordeal. Prison is no safe haven, especially when there's a price on your head."

Danny shrugged his shoulders and looked down at the table. He had never anticipated getting caught. During the war his companions referred to him as being jammy, as he always returned from the bombing raids. Only once had his plane been hit taking out an engine but they still managed to cross the English Channel, returning on three engines.

"However," added the policeman, "given the ceasefire and the Home Office having taken over the Irish problem, this might never happen. Your future might come down to a decision from higher up."

"What do you mean, might never happen?" A startled Danny looked up from the table.

"Well, given your war service and anticipated cooperation there's a possibility of repatriation to another country. You and your family would have a new identity and might live out your lives without the fear of those seeking revenge."

"Sure, and what country would want an IRA bomber?" scoffed Danny. "I think that we both know the answer to that."

"What country indeed?" smirked the policeman. "You're right. But let's just say for instance that you were never convicted and therefore didn't have a criminal record. All they'd know about is your heroism during the war and that you're no longer safe in the UK."
"Well, I've learned in this world that you never get something for nothing, so what's the catch?" Danny asked. "There's got to be a catch."

Chapter Three
Sydney, Australia
1977

"Nobody gets justice. People only get good luck or bad luck."
Orson Welles

"A grand aul day," commented Deidre as she carried two cups of tea out onto the decking where Danny, her husband, was lounging and soaking up the Sydney sun.

"I don't know what you said to the Garda in Belfast to be banished to Australia but whatever it was I'm most appreciative," she added as she placed the cups onto a table and sunk down into the other lounger. "This is so lovely just lying out here in the sunshine and this house, there are just no words to describe it after that shack in Belfast. It is so unreal and, Holy Mother of God, two jacks, one just outside our bedroom. I'll not miss that outside jack and getting a cold bum sitting on it over those cold winter nights in Belfast," laughed Deidre.

"Over here they call it an ensuite," corrected Danny. "I agree, this whole house is unreal compared to Belfast. It's so huge, and even has a large plot of land attached as well. I can now grow some spuds."

"You sure we can afford the rent Danny; this place is surely well above our income level I'd have thought?"

"Not Belfast, Deidre, my job pays very well over here in Australia. My computer skills they're in big demand," Danny drank some tea. "You know I've always been jammy."

"True that you have but what intrigues me is how you came to avoid the clink and instead earned us a one way ticket to Australia?' probed Deidre. "It just doesn't add up."

Danny paused, "Just luck and politics, Deidre, that's all. As I said, I'm jammy."

"Politics?" Deidre looked puzzled and was fishing for more details. She was like a bull terrier, once she had sunk her teeth into something there was no way she was going to let go.

Danny hesitated. He was dreading this moment. "Well ah, the Garda explained it all to me. After the British Home Office took charge of the Irish situation in 1972 everything changed."

"It got worse, tell me about it," suggested Deidre.

"Maybe," continued Danny. "But the Home Office is more concerned with the bigger picture rather than holding people accountable for their crimes and burdening the British taxpayer with more mouths to feed in prison."

"You do the crime, you do the time," interrupted Deidre. "It's what the public expects."

"True," replied Danny, "but they've found prisons to be counterproductive. They serve more as training grounds rather than the intended remorse and reform. One thing for sure, they certainly don't want bomb makers sharing their skills with other inmates." Danny nervously laughed.

"Well it never stopped them before locking up bomb makers," replied Deidre.

"Well maybe they've finally learned from their mistakes," Danny suggested as he took another sip of tea. "The Home Office," he continued, "also wants the public to believe that the Irish situation is due to a small terrorist Marxist group called the IRA, rather than dissatisfied Irish Catholics throughout Northern Ireland. The last thing they'd want the media to report on would be a war hero seen to be fighting for the cause and that Northern Ireland is in fact engaged in a civil war."

Deidre was unconvinced. She sat glaring at Danny across the table as he rose to take the empty tea cups out to the kitchen.

"What a load of bollocks!" she finally remarked, causing Danny to freeze in his tracks. "What do ya take me for, a moron? C'mere and tell me, what really happened?"

Danny reluctantly returning the cups to the table, nervously sank into his lounger, and with a big sigh began. He knew that at some stage he'd have to tell her the truth.

"Firstly, you need to know that we got caught because we were betrayed by the IRA," said Danny.

"And how would you know that?" Deidre asked.

"Well, no sooner had the bomb exploded than the Garda arrived to arrest us and they told us we'd been betrayed by the IRA."

"The IRA? Now why would they do a thing like that when you're doing their dirty work? You believe the Garda who side with the Protestants?"

"We knew too much and were expendable," replied Danny.

"Anyhow what's that got to do with you not going to the clink?" asked Deidre.

"Well, imagine the terrible things that would have happened to Sean as just a boyo in prison," appealed Danny. "It was for him, I had to take what was on offer. I had no choice."

"Ah, so you're now telling me you did a deal with the Garda and betrayed your comrádaí?" Deidre looked disgusted.

"I tell you it was to keep Sean out of prison," whimpered Danny. "Anyhow, I just helped them with their enquiries, that's all. And I wouldn't be the first in the IRA to make a deal. The Home Office was most keen to strike a deal."

"I bet they were," sniggered Deidre.

"They wanted to infiltrate the IRA before they could reform into cell groups and become a more formidable opponent," continued Danny. "They were more than happy to remove a dangerous bomb-making expert from British shores; to wash their hands clean of such terrorists. They don't want me back, that's for sure. And just remember Sean, Liam and I were betrayed first."

"So now we have both the Shankill Butchers and IRA as enemies?" suggested Deidre, "Great, thanks a million. Do we have to spend the rest of our lives looking over our shoulders?"

"Sorry, it needn't be that way, Deidre. The IRA don't know and if they did they've only themselves to blame," replied Danny. "But you're not to tell Sean any of this."

"So, that's why we have a new surname and now no friends or contacts in Ireland? We're expected to live a long and meaningful life in solitude?" suggested Deidre. "Great!"

"And the Garda also suggested that I avoid all pubs, especially those frequented by Irish expats."

"Now that I'd have to see to believe. I never thought I'd live to see the day you didn't return home banjaxed," chuckled Deidre. "But surely we owe it to my brother and your mother to let them know we're alive and well. They'll be worrying themselves sick."

"It's hard," replied Danny, "but the police said it only takes one small slip-up like that. There are people in Ireland wanting to murder us."

"Murder you. You're the one who got us into this mess," Deidre looked angry again. "Don't you bring me into it. And now we all have to suffer, though it is very nice here."

"Look!" said Danny, changing the subject. Two small lorikeets had landed on the deck railing.

"Don't you dare change the subject, you're not getting out of trouble that easily," Deidre cautioned. "You alone put us into this mess but here in Australia, I guess, we're too far away to be troubled by Loyalists and IRA seeking revenge."

"That's right, we're too far away," agreed Danny.

"And I certainly wouldn't have wanted Sean locked up," added Deidre. "He should never have been involved and I'd never have forgiven you if he had been locked up."

"Sorry, it was wrong involving Sean." Danny got up again and collected the empty tea cups to take out to the kitchen.

"Oh! Those birds are so beautiful with their mix of blue, red and green colours. What beautiful little parrots," commented Deidre. "I do love this country but it'll be hard not seeing my family and being so isolated. In Belfast everyone knew everyone on the street and we'd have many a good natters in between riots. It's just not the same here but I do love these birds, the shops and safe streets. There are also things I will miss."

"You haven't yet seen the cockatoo. They're a big parrot and quite friendly according to this man I was talking to on the harbour ferry. They often stop to visit homes, perching on the deck railings," said Danny as he took the opportunity to make his escape out to the kitchen.

Chapter Four

"All trials are trials for one's life, just as all sentences are sentences of death."
Oscar Wilde

"Top of the morning," greeted Danny as he and Deidre walked past the next door neighbour on their way down to the Cremorne jetty to catch the ferry. It was a nice healthy walk of several kilometres.

The elderly neighbour looked up speechless, giving them the once over before continuing to remove a weed entangled in his bush.

"They don't seem to be as friendly here," commented Deidre. "Though I guess we've only just moved in."

"He could have at least said good morning," commented Danny as they continued down the road to the wharf.

They didn't have long to wait before they spotted the ferry approaching in the distance from South Mosman. It didn't take long for it to arrive as it cut through the waves towards them. It only paused for a few minutes at the wharf in a sleek operation, involving the mooring and gang plank, before continuing on its way across the harbour.

"I love this," said Deidre as they sat at the back of the boat enjoying the sunshine, and fresh sea air, as well as the scenery on their journey to Circular Quay. Ahead they could see the large white shell-like structure of Sydney Opera House, staging an impressive appearance in its prominent position at the edge of the harbour with central city skyscrapers towering behind. To the right, equally impressive, arched the metallic Sydney Harbour bridge. It spanned across from the south to the north of the harbour.

"To think we can do this every day. We're very jammy," commented Deidre.

After the ferry had reached Circular Quay, both disembarked and set off on foot into town: Danny to his work and Deidre to do some window shopping.

At lunchtime Danny too was able to explore this new town, though he tried to minimize the time he spent in public areas just in case he was recognised. Even just in the short time he'd been in Sydney on occasions he had frozen in his tracks thinking he'd seen various members of the Shankill Gang walking around central Sydney. Peak periods like lunch hour were the worst. He had to remind himself that he was in Sydney, not Belfast; that when you're living amongst three million people one is bound to see someone looking vaguely familiar. One day he thought he saw big Tommy Hegarty coming out of Woolworths but, on closer inspection, he realised that once again he had been mistaken. It was going to take time to leave the past behind and accept that he was now safe.

The public library was one of the few places where he was keen to go. A safe place where he could connect with Ireland. A place where the family could keep abreast with the Irish news and it was here that Danny decided to spend his lunch breaks.

The Belfast Telegraph was a good source of Irish gossip. In particular, he had been keen to learn how successful their bombing effort had been as the Garda in Ireland deliberately denied them the satisfaction of learning the outcome of the bombing. He was equally curious to learn the fate of his accomplice, Liam O'Mahony. Had a deal been struck for him as well? Surely, if he was sentenced then it would be light, reflecting the small part he'd played in the bombing.

It was after reading the articles on the bombing and the trial that followed that he realised just how lucky they'd been and how dreadful it must have been for Liam and his family. He was pleased to see that the bombing had been successful with a number of the Shankill Butcher gang either dead or injured. Hopefully this might have a two-fold effect: to reduce the cowardly attacks by the gang on Catholics and to prompt the Garda to do their job and send these gang members to prison.

Those patrons of the pub interviewed by the press, including a badly scarred Tommy Hegarty, who described the perpetrators as a father and son with a short life expectancy. The local Protestant community had been livid at the loss of lives and the maiming of their friends and neighbours, as well as their pub being destroyed. It was abhorrent that such an attack should violate their peaceful neighbourhood. Within days following the bombing, they had risen up as a lynching mob and stormed the local constabulary demanding revenge. It became clear that Liam had to become the fall-guy and he was quickly charged for the bombing and speedily moved to more secure premises while he awaited trial. Danny believed that this would have been for the protection of the local constabulary, to protect their premises from being torched rather than for Liam's protection. It wasn't long before the mob learned Liam's address and his home was torched. Fortunately his wife and children managed to escape but lost all of their possessions. How terrible it must have been for this family.

On the day of the trial Liam was dragged from an escorted police van through a screaming mob, bruised and battered in the process of entering the courtroom. Naturally, he proclaimed his innocence saying he had neither made the bomb nor planted it in the pub. This was met with an uproar from the gallery crying "Liar, liar!", and several people were escorted out. The prosecution, on the other hand, claimed that he had switched cases; that the man and his son standing at the bar were not, as Liam had claimed, responsible as they wouldn't be so stupid as to be standing there with a bomb (unpredictable as they are) at their feet. The barman surprisingly, on cross examination, supported this argument saying the boy (Sean) was a pleasant young boyo— not the sort who'd plant a bomb. Liam, on the other hand, had presented himself in an aggressive manner and came across as the sort who would. The barman admitted that the boy shouldn't have been in the pub but the poor lad had recently lost his mother to an IRA bombing and he was accompanied by his father. The barman continued saying that he had felt sorry for the lad at losing his mother at such a young age. He was adamant that Liam was the perpetrator and must have switched the cases. The barman explained that it would have been easy for Liam to appear with a similar case to Danny, because the stocking salesman, was a regular patron and always brought along the same case. Liam obviously saw the opportunity and took it. However, for the prosecution, no witness could confirm whether or not Liam had walked in and out of the pub with a case, because at the time the pub was so packed that one couldn't even see their own feet. The police could only produce statements, which they claimed to have been taken at the time from witnesses, saying that Liam had been carrying a similar case to that left at the bar.

"So then where is the man and his boyo?" taunted the defence attorney. "They were not counted amongst the dead and surely if they were innocent then they'd be here today."

To the abhorrence of those demanding a guilty verdict, it seemed that Liam might get off scot-free on the grounds of reasonable doubt. This was until the police produced further evidence (supplied by Danny from when he brokered a deal) that Liam was a member of the IRA.

"Now tell me, what member of the IRA would seriously be foolish enough to walk into a Protestant pub just for a pint of Guinness, frequented by a gang known by the name of the Shankill Butchers,?" asked the prosecution.

"Check mate!" yelled a man in the gallery, and it was.

The newspaper reported that Liam, to the delight of the gallery, was unanimously found guilty and sentenced to several life imprisonments. He left the court loudly proclaiming his innocence and was sent to the Maze prison. On reading this, Danny feared for Liam's wellbeing, imprisoned with notorious Protestant psychopaths. At the same time he hoped the Shankill Butchers had believed the prosecution's account of events; that Liam had acted alone. It was a sobering thought for Danny and made him even more confident that they could now move on with their lives without worrying over reprisals.

Chapter Five
Sydney 1982

'It is easy enough to be pleasant,
When life flows by like a song,
But the man worthwhile
is one who will smile,
When everything goes dead wrong."
Ella Wheeler Wilcox

One day, Danny was reading one of the Irish newspapers at the library when he froze in shock. Tears streamed down his cheek as he read a public notice advising of his mother's death and the intention to distribute her estate. At the time this was most disturbing news to Danny. He had been close to his mother and had been most unhappy about severing his contact with her following the bombing. His mother had understood though and was proud of her son for once again putting his body on the line for freedom. She told him that his family mattered and he needed to break all contact with other family members. Many times he had wanted to phone her but he always managed to resist the temptation. He would have liked to have been with her and the priest on her deathbed as she drew her last breath. It was hard having to ostracise oneself, especially from family members, but it was essential and he knew she understood. The inheritance situation was straightforward. As the only child all he needed to do was to claim his inheritance. It was quite a substantial amount, being the proceeds from the sale of his mother's house. Danny was indeed lucky as this windfall came at a time when they needed money to purchase their own house in Sydney. He wrote to the solicitor in Ireland claiming his inheritance and after a number of weeks involving exchanges of information and evidence, the solicitor confirmed that there would be a fat cheque in the mail.

"Today's the day," announced Danny as he bounced out of the house to go to work. "It's a beautiful sunny day and I feel jammy, Deidre. I just have that feeling that today the cheque will be there."
"And pigs might fly," laughed Deidre. "This isn't the first day you've had that feeling. Have a grand aul day," she shouted after him as he strode down the street to the ferry. "Now that's one very happy man," she said, turning to Sean, who nodded in agreement.
Danny planned on checking his postal box after work as he had no plans to carry a cheque of that amount around all day. Having a post box rather than

mail delivered to their street address had been advised for their own safety. Now all their mail was directed to a postal box in central Sydney. Danny had visited this box now for the last four days in anticipation of this cheque arriving but each time he left disappointed.

After work he once again strode down the skyscraper-lined George Street, ever hopeful that today would be the day. It was one of those hot muggy days, and everybody seemed to be going home or out shopping, as he ambled down George Street. It was of course peak hours with people starting to leave for home. He felt optimistic as he headed towards his post box. On the way he passed Tommy Hegarty's look alike who must work nearby.

"Hello Tommy." He cheekily provoked as he frisked past in a jovial mood. The large man turned slowly and glared disconcertingly at Danny who, with a chuckle, continued on his way. The thought struck him that he'd never get away with that had it been the real Tommy Hegarty but then he could still outrun the big man.

Just down the road was the old white concrete building, housing his postal box. He cheerfully continued down the street, somewhat expecting to find a nice fat cheque waiting for him. It would be a game changer. At the post office he pressed his way through a number of other people blocking the entrance way, also keen to check their postal boxes. Danny located his box and optimistically turned the key. This time there it was, a long brown envelope and it was from the solicitor in Belfast. It had to be because apart from electricity bills they got little other mail. He excitedly removed and examined the cheque, smiling at the huge amount, before securely placing it into his pocket. They had never owned or been able to afford their own house before. Deidre would be ecstatic now no longer having to rent. She had already found a number of houses she liked in anticipation. It had been great fun looking around at houses observing the luxuriant lifestyle Australians led.

Danny was so deep in thought, pondering these possibilities as he left his post box that he almost bumped into a solidly built red-headed man standing outside the building. It wasn't until he had walked further down the pavement that he froze in his tracks and slowly and apprehensively turned to look back. Was this just another look-a-like of somebody from his past? There, standing outside the building watching everyone going in and out was Shane Gallagher and another man. He looked hard again. There was no doubting it this time, the man was definitely Shane. Had the cheque been worth it and how on earth had they found him he wondered? It was inconceivable, how anyone other than the solicitor could have learned of his whereabouts. Perhaps it was the public notice and a phone call to the solicitor's office or simply just a coincidence that an acquaintance of Shane Gallagher worked for the solicitor. Whatever the explanation, it was still a mystery and seemed impossible.

Once again Danny had been lucky managing to empty his box without being seen but he now feared that his luck had run out. Shane was with a much younger man wearing a green shirt. As he continued to look back, to his horror, Shane turned his head and suddenly their eyes met. Immediately Shane's face lit with rage but by then Danny had taken to his heels weaving between pedestrians down a busy George Street pavement. He had never run so fast in his life. Although he felt sweat collecting and his heart pounding, and knew this was not wise at his age, this was not the time to stop or slow down. The enraged red-headed Irishman shouting profanities and shaking his fist followed in pursuit, uncaringly shoving aside pedestrians in his way. Fortunately Shane's colleague was slow to react but once he did, being much younger and fitter, he soon overtook Shane and was closing in fast. Danny realized it would only be a matter of time before he was apprehended. His life now depended on using his local knowledge of the area to outsmart them.

Danny decided to chance his arm as he was as good as dead anyway. He recklessly crossed a traffic-packed George Street where cars were lined up, the lights due to change any second. On either side of him sat eager Sydney drivers with feet hung expectantly over their accelerators poised to respond once the lights turned green. He managed to sprint to the other side, barely making it as the Daytona checkered flag fell. His pursuers could only stop and watched the traffic racing by while Danny regained ground on the other side. He had now bought enough time, with his pursuers unable to cross the road. But they decided instead to keep up with Danny by running along the other side waiting for a break in the traffic to cross. Meanwhile, Danny headed for the Queen Victoria Building where he hoped that he might outsmart them. This grand old nineteenth century building with four floors of shops was, as he anticipated, packed with shoppers, tourists and commuters, plenty to get lost amongst. He speedily weaved his way through the crowds and through a food court, somewhat popular at this time of day, and headed down towards the basement and the underground train station. As luck would have it, a Sydney intercity train was about to leave. As the train pulled away, he nervously peered back through the window. His pursuers had not come into sight but would probably guess he'd taken a train. It appeared that he had been successful in losing them. Now with his heart still pounding and the sweat still dripping off his forehead from both the adrenaline rush and the Sydney humidity, he tried to sit calmly and restore his physical condition to some degree of normality. But it was to no avail as his heart continued to pound deeply and rapidly and he continued to sweat profusely. His handkerchief served little purpose as no sooner had he mopped up the sweat on his forehead than more appeared.

"Are you OK?" a concerned passenger asked him.

"Just not used to the Sydney humidity," replied an out of breath Danny.

"Oh, Irish. Yes, it is somewhat hotter here," replied the lady. "And I guess it doesn't help when you have to run to catch the train. The doors don't seem to stay open for long."

When the train arrived at Circular Quay he hastily left, taking to the stairs at the station. At the bottom of the stairway he stopped and apprehensively looked back. Thankfully the only other person descending was a mother with two young children. Now satisfied that he hadn't been followed, he moved quickly towards the ferry terminal. It was nice to feel the cooler air coming off the sea but he had no time to just stand there and enjoy the cool breeze. Before proceeding he quickly scanned the area, checking that there were no more unexpected surprises.

Circular Quay turned out to be a good choice as it provided many ferries leaving for different destinations across Sydney Harbour. Even if his pursuers somehow learned that he had gone to Circular Quay they would still need to know which boat he'd taken and where he'd disembarked. Danny proceeded to the wharf and by sheer luck there was the Mosman Ferry close to leaving. He boarded the large boat, finding a seat outside at the back which gave him a view of the wharf area as well as exposure to the cool refreshing sea breeze. He was still dripping profusely and his shirt now felt damp.
"Hurry up," he mumbled as he watched one of the crew waiting for a straggler in a green shirt to board. Finally the ferrymen removed the gangplank giving him the assurance that he was safe and hadn't been followed. Shortly afterwards the ferry gave a few jerks then slowly inched away from the wharf and Circular Quay. Docked across the far side of

Circular Quay was a massive cruise ship which had not long arrived. Danny would have, in other circumstances, given it much more attention but his mind was on more concerning things and unpopular decisions that might need to be made.

The ferry headed diagonally to the left after passing the famous white shell building of the Sydney Opera house. Out in the harbour it was windy and cooler, so Danny moved into the ship's cabin where most of the other passengers were seated. The boat continued to cross the harbour towards Cremorne point, a narrow piece of land reaching out into the harbour. This was the first stop for the ferry and where Danny had planned to disembark. Extending into Sydney harbour the Cremorne floating wharf is exposed to wind and choppy seas and on this particular day the wind was wild and the wharf bobbed up and down as the ferry rolled alongside. The crewman quickly managed to secure a rope to the wharf and draw the boat in closer. He placed a gangplank between the boat and wharf. Even with the one hand rail, disembarking did not look straightforward nor safe with it bouncing about. After his ordeal, was Danny now to simply die falling off a gangplank into the turbulent waters between the boat and wharf? He and three other passengers lined up to leave the boat. The first, a middle-aged woman with the crewman's assistance nervously made it onto the wharf. Next it was Danny's turn. He confidently stepped onto the plank but before he could take another step he felt a push from behind.

"Oops, sorry," muttered a voice behind him.

"Look out!" The crewman grabbed Danny's arm until he was able to steady himself.

"That was close," commented Danny, realizing he had been in danger of falling into the choppy waters.

The middle-aged man who had pushed him from behind looked shaky and also required a lot of assistance. It was the first time Danny had seen him on the boat and he reminded him of somebody in the Shankill Butcher's gang but he couldn't remember who. Could this just be another look alike and was the push just a case of this man being unsteady on his feet? The fourth to disembark was a young man amused by the incident, who flatly refused assistance and looked to be trying to impress some young women watching on the boat. It seemed that he had done this many times. All four passengers left the wharf and walked up the steep adjoining road where they were met by a bus. Living in Cremorne had been Danny's choice since it was serviced by both ferry and bus and was not too far from North Sydney where he could also use rail. Sea, road and rail provided a choice for escape routes for the family should such a situation like this arise.

At the first stop the middle-aged woman left the bus. Danny could not believe how lazy people could be when the stop was only a few hundred yards up the road. This left the young man in his twenties and the middle-aged man as the only other people who had left the ferry. At the next stop the older of the men left. Only Danny and the younger man remained. Danny was now convinced that he had only the younger man in the green shirt to worry about. Could this be the same young man who was with Shane? The problem was that he'd never had time to observe the other man at the postal centre, so he had no idea what he looked like apart from his green shirt. To be on the safe side Danny decided to continue on the bus passing his house. He would leave the bus instead at the supermarket on Military Road. Now perhaps it was just coincidence but the young man seemed to have the same idea. Danny decided to enter the supermarket and see if he'd follow. The young man did not and when Danny left the supermarket there was no sign of him. Danny continued home but taking an indirect route just as a safeguard. Occasionally he'd look back to see that he wasn't followed. Finally, exhausted, he reached the door of his house.

Chapter Six

"While seeking revenge, dig two graves- one for yourself."
Douglas Horton

"Holy Mother of God!" A frightened Deidre exclaimed at her husband's belligerent entry as he burst through the door, slamming and locking it behind him.

"You alright?"

"Knackered", mumbled a bedraggled Danny, flushed and sweaty with his shirt tail following behind him as he rushed across to the window overlooking the street in front of his house. He was a real mess and not the picture of the calm, cheerful, immaculately dressed husband who had set out for work that morning. Danny caught his breath as the sweat once again started to roll down his face.

"They've found us. Bloody hell, they're here, said Danny looking out the window."

"Who?" asked Deidre.

"The Shankill Butchers," replied a terrified Danny who was now sweating profusely.

"What, outside our house, here in Australia? You're off your trolley." Deidre quipped. "Come on, nobody knows we're here in Australia. We've been here for a few years and nobody knows."

"I saw him, Deidre, the red-headed moron they call Knuckles. He was lurking outside near my post box down George Street."

"A look-alike, just like your Tommy Hegarty, that's all," laughed Deidre. "Sydney's a big city and you're bound to find faces and bodies of similar looks, shapes and sizes. Get over it, we have a new life. Nobody could possibly know we've moved here, sadly not even family."

"They chased me down George Street but I think I lost them," added Danny as he continued to observe the roadside outside their house.

"Sorry, they chased you, now are you sure?" Deidre looked surprised. "Probably just walking in the same direction. It happens a lot."

"Holy Mother of God, look they chased me!" repeated Danny. "I should know."

"Did they take the same ferry, train or whatever you took to get home then?"

"Well, not that I know of," replied Danny, "but that's because I managed to lose them I think."

"Look, how would they even know we're in Sydney; we told nobody?"

"I know, I wondered that too. Look, here's the proceeds from Ma's estate." Danny produced the cheque from his pocket. "Maybe they got wind of it through my communication with the solicitor."

Deidre snatched the cheque out of Danny's hand. "A load of baloney. You sure you're not fluthered?"

"I haven't touched a drop of the black stuff since we left Ireland," replied an indignant Danny, "but a jar would surely go down nicely now to calm my nerves."

"What's all the commotion? I'm trying to study!" complained Sean, entering the room. He had been studying in his bedroom. "Da's not pissed again? Thought he'd given up the black stuff for good since we came to Australia."

"Your dad says he was chased by the Shankill Butchers," laughed Deidre. "Can you believe it, here in Australia – the other side of the world?"

"What, here in Australia? Impossible" laughed Sean. "He's surely pissed."

"That's my thinking," replied Deidre. "But he claims he was chased through town."

"It was that red-headed thug called Knuckles and a younger man." Danny had regained some composure.

"They'd come all this way from Ireland to settle a score?" asked Sean. "I don't believe it. That red-headed moron was a nasty piece from memory though. Hopefully he was blown into many pieces when that bomb went off. I hope they all were."

"That's not nice talk, Sean" commented Deidre.

"They deserved it," replied Sean. "We should have just made a bigger bomb."

"Sean!" Deidre chided.

"Not that impossible," replied Danny. "Sydney's just a day or two by plane from Belfast."

"Sit down before your ticker gives out and you overwork your brain trying to explain your behaviour. You better have a cup of tea or there'll be nil Danny to murder," Deidre said, laughing as she sauntered off to the kitchen. "Shankill Butchers! The man's surely losing his marbles."

Danny sank into a seat near the window where he could keep watch if anyone came up the path.

"You know it means we're going to have to move again," declared Danny.

"I like this place and we're staying," replied his stubborn wife from the kitchen, "and we can now buy our own house and we will and I know where." She stroked the cheque in her hand. Never before had she seen so much money. "Just a senior moment, that's all it is, Danny. Happens to us all, obviously some sooner than others though. Hope you're not coming down with a bad dose of dementia." Deirdre laughed again.

"I'm not codding you, it happened. They somehow found out we're here in Sydney," said Danny.

"You'll be a different man tomorrow, mark my words. A good night's kip that's what you need," reassured Deidre as she brought Danny his cup of tea. "Now drink this up then change your clothes, just in case they have sniffer dogs tracking you," she laughed again.

"I'm in the middle of school exams and I'm staying," said Sean. "I'm not leaving my friends behind this time, that's for sure. Not this time."

"Then we'll move after the exams," Danny picked up his cup of tea with his shaky left hand and had a sip. "Your exams are important."

"Move to where?" asked Deidre. "I like Sydney. I like the shops and to be able to walk down the road without soldiers, barriers and checkpoints. It's nice to know that here somebody isn't going to throw a brick through your window. One thing's for sure, we won't be moving back to Belfast."

"I do miss my friends in Belfast, though," sighed Sean, returning to his room. "I miss my cousin Paddy."

"We all miss our friends and family there," replied Deidre.

Danny finished his cup of tea, eager to shower and change into some clean clothes.

The next day Danny called in sick. He didn't want to go anywhere near town and was frightened to even go out to the local Cremorne shops on Military Road.

"You're going to have to go back to work sometime," said Deidre. You can't just keep calling in sick because you've suddenly developed a bad case of paranoia."

"I know, but it's a case of buying time. Sooner or later they're sure to find out where we live and we don't want to be here when that happens. I'm thinking about going out later to report the incident to the police."

"And what will they do Danny?" asked Deidre. "Were you assaulted and where are your witnesses? They'll be as useless as the Garda in Ireland. They're only interested in drug cases and murder. They're bound to think you're off your trolley and they'll not be on their own. They might even send the men in white to take you away," laughed Deidre.

"It's better than waiting for a bullet," replied Danny.

Several days later Danny returned to work and handed in his resignation, taking effect after Sean had finished his exams. Travelling to and from work was not as simple now. Danny avoided main streets like George and Pitt Streets and the railway stations scattered around the town and instead opted for a longer journey involving many small streets. It was not just the red-headed man Danny was worried about now as he suspected that Knuckles would have employed private detectives to track him down. If they knew to find him in Sydney then they must be aware of their surname change. Fortunately their name would be on few public records as they owned neither a car nor house. But there were other records such as power bills where they had to use their new name. Now every person who dared look at him or follow him he considered suspicious. Of course his furtive appearance drew suspicious stares. In turn this contributed to his paranoia. It was a case of moving briskly to and from work and checking that he hadn't been followed.

Danny bounced home that Friday much happier and relieved that he had completed the week without incident. He felt confident that for the next week or two they remained safe. He was greeted at the door by a somewhat distressed Sean.

"Da, I'm sorry. I believe you now," he said.

An equally worried Deidre looked on but this time remained silent.

"Believe me concerning what?" asked Danny.

"About Knuckles being here," replied Sean. "I saw him in town too."

"Did he see you?" Danny looked concerned.

"I'm no longer the skinny thirteen-year-old he'd recognize," said Sean. "And I was also with some other tall boys."

"Were you followed?" asked Danny.

"I don't think he even noticed me though at one stage he was looking our way," Sean said. "Don't worry, I continued to act naturally and never caught his eye. I wasn't followed, I'm sure of that."

"Was anyone with him?" Danny asked.
"Not sure but then I didn't look hard after I spotted him." Sean looked concerned. "I think you're right and we need to leave Sydney."

"For where?" asked Deirdre. "Do we have to keep running all our lives? Maybe we can go and join Colleen in Perth. I like Australia and I'm sure it will be just as nice there."

"We don't want to endanger our daughter's life as well," replied Danny. "I was thinking maybe Auckland in New Zealand. I've already booked our flights."

"Auckland?" Deirdre replied.

"You'll like it there, it won't be as humid though and when it rains it buckets down, just like Belfast."

Chapter Seven

Christchurch, New Zealand 2022

"Keep love in your heart. A life without it is like a sunless garden when the flowers are dead."

Oscar Wilde

"Top of the mornin' to you, Susie Wong," greeted Sean O'Brien. Have you found any leprechauns yet in that garden of yours?

The elderly Chinese lady raised her head above the roses which she had been pruning. Fortunately she had a raised garden and was able, despite her shortness, to look over the paling fence.

"Leprechauns?" She looked rather perplexed. Was this some sort of noxious weed that she needed to pull out?

"Ignore him, he's just being rude. He's just referring to the amount of time you spend in that garden of yours," Sergeant said.

"Leprechaun are part of our Irish folklore. They're magical little people that hide in nooks and crannies of the garden. If you catch one you can make a wish," explained Sean. "By now you must have found one or two, maybe even a family?"

Sergeant laughed. She enjoyed Sean's droll sense of humour but sometimes he was over the top.

"Morning, Mr. Sean. Morning, Sergeant. You funny man, Mr. Sean. I spray my garden then to kill those Leprechaun. Didn't see Sergeant arrive this morning," Susie probed.

She was a nosey one that needed to know everything that was happening. They suspected that it was probably why she spent so much time out there in her front garden neglecting the jungle that was once a vegetable garden behind her house.
"I can assure you that we're just good friends," replied an embarrassed Sean. "You're the lady of my life," he teased.

"Sure, tell me another one." Susie grinned. "You Irishmen all alike."

"His name should have been Sean O'Flattery," joked Sergeant.

"I hear that there's been big military operations in the China Sea. Is China going to invade Taiwan?" teased Sean.

"Invade?" Susie shook her head. "Why invade Taiwan when already province of China? Oh, I noticed same black van parked across road." Susie said, changing the subject. She now looked worried.

"Did you see who was in it?" Sean asked. "A man or woman, young or old and how many?"

"No, window tinted," replied Susie. "Who are they? What they want?"

"Never-mind Susie, it's more than likely a private detective employed by my ex. She's wanting more out of her share of the matrimonial property. I've had her on my back now for several years asking for more. That woman always was a gold digger. This time she probably heard that I've made good sales from my latest novel," laughed Sean. "She never got over it when I told her my great, great grandfather was Gabriel and I had a map to where he was getting all his gold."

"You didn't? How could you?" Sergeant looked shocked, then gave Sean a friendly shove. "No, you rat-bag you're having us on again. I think he must have kissed that Blarney stone, Susie."

"Blarney Stone?" Susie queried.

"Never been to Blarney Castle in my life" laughed Sean. "Didn't need to."

"No, you certainly didn't," replied Sergeant. "You were already born with the gift of the gab."

"Well she married me for something other than my good looks," laughed Sean.
"Who are you trying to kid? What good looks?" teased Sergeant.

"Gold? What gold? Who's Gabriel?" asked Susie, lost in the conversation. "Where's this gold?"

"Oh it goes back to the gold rush in Central Otago over a hundred years ago, Susie. Gabriel seemed to return with bucket loads of gold but nobody ever found out where he was mining it. They think it was in a gully they now call Gabriel's Gully," replied Sergeant. "But don't believe him, Susie. He's telling lies again. Anyhow, what's this about someone spying on you?"
Sergeant, who was a policewoman, looked concerned.

"It's not what you're thinking," replied Sean, referring to his Irish past. "That episode in my life has long gone for sure."

"Oh, I'm not so sure." Sergeant started to amble down the path towards her car as a small blue Nissan March pulled up.

"What do you mean?" asked Sean.

"We need to keep tabs on this. If you can get a car number plate then maybe I can find out more," offered Sergeant.

"Hello, here's Holy Joe," announced Sean.

The driver's door on the Nissan March sprung open and a balding middle-aged man stepped out.

"Howya, police sergeant, Sean and Susie," he greeted in an Irish accent.

"Top of the mornin' to you, Father," replied Sean.

"And the rest of the day to you," replied Father Ted.

"Here, I noted down the car number," Susie reached into her pocket and handed Sergeant a scrunched up scrap of paper.

"I'll see what I can do," replied Sergeant as she bent down to get into her car.

"So what might all this be about?" the Father asked. Like Susie, he seemed to want to know about everyone else's business.
"Nothing really, you don't need to know," replied Sergeant dismissively.

"Somebody appears to be spying on us and Sergeant thinks that…"

"No, Sean I wouldn't go there," Sergeant warned. "Kia whakatōmuri te haere whakamua."

"Meaning…?" Sean asked.

"It's a Māori proverb; I walk backwards into the future with my eyes fixed on the past," Sergeant replied. "There should be enough reason in the past, if you think about it, to remain silent."

"Holy Mother of God, I'm a priest and hear about all sorts of sensitive issues in confessions, Sergeant. I'm sure I could solve many of your crime cases but my lips, as a priest, remain sealed. Not one word passes by. Anything Sean tells me will remain confidential."

Sergeant shook her head. "Say nothing," she shouted out her window as she drove off. Ever since Sean had come to Christchurch she had been given the responsibility of monitoring his safety, especially after what had happened to other family members.

"Tell me Sean, I've always wondered, you're the best of friends so why do you never call her by her first name?" Father Ted looked surprised.

"It is her first name," replied Sean as they walked to the house. "Her father was a policeman and he called her Sergeant as he could never see himself rising to the rank of sergeant. She said that at the time the force was pretty racist and Māori were held back from promotion. Ironically, to her father's delight, she became a real Sergeant."

"Oh dear, so many injustices in this world but as you can see over time they do get sorted," replied the priest. "All we can do is pray for a fairer world."

Father Ted and Sean made their way inside, leaving a curious Susie in her garden more than ever eager to learn more about the hidden chapters of Sean's life.

"So tell me what's all this about?" persisted the priest holding up a cup of tea in his right hand. "Has it anything to do with Ireland?"

"Susie thinks that somebody is spying on me," answered Sean. "Sergeant thinks it may have something to do with Ireland."

"Which was?" asked the priest.

Sean remained silent.

"Look," said the tenacious priest, "I'm a priest, you know you can trust me. I've suspected for some time you may have some sort of troubling Irish history given the way you tend to keep to yourself and never mix with other Irish expats." Father Ted looked at Sean. "Please, you can share your problem with me and perhaps it's something we can pray about."

Sean swallowed his mouthful of tea, still somewhat apprehensive about sharing his past, especially with another Irishman.

"Well, being Irish you'll remember those early days in Northern Ireland were pretty turbulent," he began.

"Do I ever? Chaotic, would be a better description," said the Father. "They were sad times indeed and they thought the potato famine was bad. How families managed to survive was a miracle."

"Bang on! It was not a particularly pleasant situation and one most of us Catholics found hard to tolerate," continued Sean.

"Indeed," confirmed the priest. "Catholics were oppressed. We were treated badly."

"Oppressed! They were treated more like dirt, as second-rate citizens and in our own country." Sean picked up his cup of tea with a shaky hand and struggled to take a sip to calm his nerves.

"Don't I know it," replied Father Ted. "Believe me, in Ireland it wasn't that much better, though I felt for those of you in the North and the turmoil you had to endure. Those were indeed terrible days."

"Then there was the annual Orange Day March passing by Catholic Streets. Our street had to be barricaded to stop drunken marchers storming down and pitching bricks and fire bombs through our windows," continued an agitated Sean. "It had happened before."

Father Ted reached across and patted Sean on his back to console him.

"It wasn't much fun living on a barricaded street," continued Sean "and even as a child, being frisk searched and interrogated by English soldiers. They wouldn't even allow children to play on the street." Sean seemed quite upset by his childhood memories. "The morons stole my childhood." He took another mouthful of tea before continuing.
"It was not a happy time and those marches were very provocative and should never have been allowed."

"Agreed," said the priest. "And the St Patrick marches, with the IRA out in full force, weren't?"

"That's not the same Father, when you have unpredictable drunk Protestants on a rampage down your street. Our houses might not have been much to talk about but they're all we had."

"I understand, it must have been hard for you," replied Father Ted, trying to calm Sean down. "You know, but I've often thought about the irony here."

"And what would that be, Father?"

"Well on one hand you have those wanting to remain part of England having a Dutchman, William of Orange, as their hero. On the other hand the IRA and others who want to break away from England, their hero is St Patrick, an Englishman. Now how Irish can that be?"

"St Patrick, an Englishman? Really?" Sean looked surprised.

"Indeed our patron saint was," replied the Father.

"Then there was Bloody Sunday in Derry in 1972," continued an upset Sean. "Catholics were out in force, exercising their legal rights in a peaceful protest for civil rights when British soldiers fired upon them. We were doing nothing wrong. It was all legal and the scum murdered fourteen unarmed protesters. Such a cowardly act, not only shooting unarmed protesters but also shooting them in the back when they were fleeing the scene. And have the soldiers ever been held accountable, Father?"
"Not that I know of," replied the priest. "So have they?"

"Never," continued Sean.

"Oh dear." The priest looked saddened. "That is a travesty of justice."

"They were all exonerated by the British government, probably quietly promoted and upheld as heroes. It was then that many of us concluded that the politicians couldn't be trusted and the only pathway to a fairer society was through violence." Sean took another mouthful of tea and paused.

"Oh dear, not violence?" The priest looked upset.

"The IRA ranks swelled and shootings and bombings became endemic. Then there was the case more recently when Margaret Thatcher allowed hunger strikers to die. How could anyone be so callous?" Sean very shakily managed to pick up his cup and sip some more tea.

"Indeed they were sad times but violence is never the answer," Father Ted replied calmly, again patting Sean on the back. "Violence only leads to more violence and violence to revenge. Change can be achieved through peaceful means. Jesus was similarly a radical fighting the establishment but he said to love your enemies and to render unto Caesar the things that are Caesars."

"That's all very well, but look where he ended up, being crucified," added Sean. "Then not long after all that the Romans sacked Jerusalem."

"Ah! But if you read your bible, you'd know that it was God's plan for him to pay the price for our sins. Jesus expected to die. The prophet Isaiah, centuries before, foretold exactly what transpired. Sean, change often takes time requiring little steps so we need to be patient rather than resorting to violence when we can't get our own way. Besides, you refer to it as a Catholic-Protestant conflict when it was in fact a struggle between the nationalists who wanted union with Ireland and the loyalists who wanted to remain as part of the UK."

"Same thing," stormed Sean. "There's no difference."

"But there is," disputed Father Ted. "It just so happens that most loyalists are Protestant and most nationalists are Catholic but I'm sure there were some Catholic who wanted to remain British and some Protestants who wanted to be part of a united Ireland."

"That wasn't my experience," replied Sean.

"That's because Catholics and Protestants sharing a different view were fearful of expressing it, lest they were beaten up or murdered. I heard one story about a Protestant taxi driver, who had been driving both Protestant and Catholic patrons home from the pub, being threatened and warned by loyalists not to transport Catholics," added the Father. "Unfortunately, the struggle even to this day has been portrayed by many as being religious but even religion in name is not Christianity. Tell me, do you recall Shane O'Doherty, the most notorious IRA bomber who planted bombs around London and mailed letter bombs, to even ten Downing Street?"

"Certainly, now he's one of my heroes," replied Sean. "A great man who fought for change and he made some great bombs."

"Well, it may have taken a period in prison, but he finally came to the realisation that violence would never lead to change. He became a Christian and a voice in Ireland for change through peaceful means. In fact he became a priest," said Father Ted.

"Well, not all priests saw peace as the answer," replied Sean. "Father Chesney was suspected of being the IRA director of operations in South Derry and involved in the Claudy bombing where three car bombs went off simultaneously killing nine people."

"A terrible, terrible situation indeed," replied Father Ted. "I remember that but recall that when questioned by his Bishop, Father Chesney denied all involvement. The Catholic Church was never supportive of IRA activities and despite the jury being out on his involvement, they had him transferred away from the troubled areas just in case. Anyhow, you haven't told me yet why you might be under surveillance. What did you do?" persisted the priest.

Sean paused, he really didn't want to tell Father too much.
"Nothing really. I was just a lad of about thirteen in Belfast at the time but I suspect that my father had a part to play in IRA activities."

"There were many a good man and lad drawn into the IRA in those days," said Father Ted. "I am surprised though if you had no involvement as many teenagers carried out IRA dirty work. Shane O'Doherty joined the IRA at fifteen years of age. There were even twelve and thirteen year olds drawn into the conflict and killed in action. So, what did your dad do to make it necessary to move to the other side of the world?"

"Really, I don't know," lied Sean.

"Then why, might I ask, would anyone be out to get you, then?" Father Ted enquired. "It would seem a rather drastic action for anyone from the other side of the world to hunt down an innocent lad don't you think?"

"If you remember at the time, Father, there were some pretty murderous, sadistic thugs in the Ulster Loyalist gangs. They had murdered and assaulted many Catholics. If you rocked their boat then there's no telling to what level they'd take revenge. They were even known to kill their own."

"Protestants?" Father Ted picked up his cup of tea.

"Correct. Those they believed had betrayed them or did not support them," replied Sean.

"Well!" exclaimed Father Ted, "I'd have thought you'd have to play some significant part to draw anybody seeking revenge from the other side of the world. Have you been to confession and sought forgiveness for the part your family played?"

"What! Seek forgiveness from those murderous thugs? You've got to be kidding."

"No, from God," the priest calmly replied.

"Look, I carry no remorse for anything that happened. They got everything they deserved," growled Sean. "Nothing would make me happier than knowing they were all blown to smithereens."

"Oh dear," replied the priest, looking quite shocked and concerned.

"But you're not to tell Sergeant any of our conversation, Father. All the authorities here know is that my father was a war hero and we were relocated to another country for our own protection."

"Sean, I'm a priest. What you confess to me is held in confidence. Now tell me, how did you come to be in New Zealand?"

Chapter Eight

"Who controls the past controls the future. Who controls the present controls the past."

Orson Welles

"**N**ow that's a long story." Sean took another sip of tea, to calm down, before continuing. "Initially we moved to Australia. Da was very good with electronics and the early eighties was a time when personal computers and home electronic kits were in their infancy and very popular. Initially, the oul fella was employed with the Dick Smith chain. Their System 80 computer was very popular, having twice the capacity of their competitors. 16K, would you believe it, when today we talk about terabytes? And the software was cassette tapes and the language: Basic."

"My memory goes back even further before the transistor," laughed Father Ted reminiscing. "As a boy I made myself a crystal set so I could listen to the radio at night. Didn't require much, just a copper coil, diode, earphones and you used the old metal bed springs as an aerial. I used to like lying in bed listening to the rugby when Ireland and the Lions were playing the All Blacks in New Zealand and the Spring Boks in South Africa. Those were the days. We had a good team then and we have a good team now."

"It was great fun," Sean agreed. "Da's skills were highly sought after and we comfortably settled down to our new life. He also got very well paid and had started saving hard for a house of our own. It seemed that we had shaken off the past and we were certainly looking towards a bright future but as we found out that was not the case. We were lured into a false sense of security. The Oul Fella, one day realised he had made a mistake when he claimed his inheritance after his mother died."

"A mistake? I'm sure that the money at the time would have come in very handy," Father Ted commented. "Did you have much money when you left for Australia?"
"Nothing," replied Sean. "We were bundled out in the middle of the night with virtually the clothes on our backs."
"Oh dear, a covert operation?" suggested the Father.

"Correct," replied Sean. "It had to be, with no questions asked or goodbyes given."

"That money would have come in as very useful then," replied the Father.

"It did and I guess it wasn't what you'd call a mistake but was just very bad luck and most unlike Da who had been jammy all his life. How the murderous Unionists had learned of our whereabouts remains a mystery to this day. Nevertheless, they did and were monitoring the public post box where Da had directed our mail. When Da arrived home one day he was in bits having had to flee through the Sydney business area for his life with those morons in pursuit. He arrived home hot and sweaty and we feared he might have a heart attack."

"Oh dear me," commented the priest. "It must have been so terrible for you."

"Actually, to tell you the truth, we didn't believe him; that the murderous thugs had found him – well not then. Like you, we thought it ludicrous that they would pursue us to the ends of the earth."

"That indeed was exactly my thoughts," confirmed Father Ted.

"We actually thought he was fluthered. He was a true Irishman, not impartial to a jar or two of the black stuff. It was hard to believe when we moved to Australia and were avoiding public places, that he'd given it up."

"Nothing at all wrong with having a drop of the black stuff now and again though," laughed the Father. "Makes for good medicine on a cold winter's day." The Father licked his lips at the thought of a pint.

"That night he never went to bed. Just sat by the window all night peering out waiting for a red-headed moron called Shane Gallagher to appear. The next few days he pulled sickies until he managed to regain confidence to return to his job in town. He was a right mess and all that time we didn't believe him, not one little bit. Shameful but we weren't at all sympathetic towards the oul fella. He was a good dad though and wanted me to complete my high school education first so we remained in Sydney with plans in the pipeline for a relocation to New Zealand after my exams. Meanwhile, Da went to great lengths changing his appearance. He grew a moustache, dyed his hair, and wore glasses and different clothes. I think that his workmates must have concluded, like we did, that he'd suddenly gone off his trolley. He was no longer the Danny they or we had come to know and like."

"Even just over several weeks he looked quite different?" asked Father Ted.

"Did he ever!" laughed Sean. "He also handed in his notice and asked for a reference. After all those years of no jobs or poorly paid jobs in Ireland and here he was resigning from a well-paying job. Ma was furious."

"Indeed she would be," commented the priest.

"Our flight was booked to Auckland where he told Mum that he was sure of getting a job with computers because people with his electronic knowledge were scarce at that time. Meanwhile he was very careful to minimise his time in public areas, especially when he was travelling to and from work. Sydney is a big city, easy to get lost in and everything seemed to work out well. At the time that's what we thought."

"And he never saw the red-headed man again?" asked the priest.

"Well, I did. It was then that I knew my dad hadn't gone off his trolley. It was Shane Gallagher for sure and he looked as menacing as ever," replied Sean. "I couldn't help myself. When I saw him I just stared and stared in disbelief. I lied to Da that he never saw me but he did."

"Oh dear, now why did you lie to your dad, Sean?" asked the concerned Father.

"It wasn't nice seeing Da in bits and this would have troubled him immensely knowing that the problem hadn't gone away and now I too was in great danger. I didn't want him to know where I saw him."

"Why?" asked the priest.

"At the time I believed the oul fella was fluthered, so I disregarded his instruction to keep away from public places like pubs. If Da could still drink at pubs then so could I. One rule fits all."

"Oh dear! Now this is where parenting falls apart," commented the priest. "Children follow the examples of their parents, not their instructions."

"Anyhow, my friends had been pressing me to join them for a drink. In Ireland I was too young to drink but then in Australia when I reached the legal age my dad told me I couldn't. Several of my friends found an Irish pub. It was an opportunity to down a jar of black stuff for the first time. I also longed to be amongst Irish people and hear Irish music again. I had missed Ireland so much."

"Oh, I love Molly Malone," interrupted Father Ted. "There's nothing like Irish music."

"Indeed," Sean agreed, then continued. "We found this Irish pub in the central city. It was great, a little like the pubs in Ireland but nowhere near as old and lacking the same rustic character. After we were seated at a table and enjoying ourselves I was looking around and noticed three men sitting at a table towards the back of the room. They were drinking Guinness and two of the men had red hair. Immediately Shane Gallagher, that moron, sprang to mind. I looked again and I got the shock of my life as the older one lifted his head. It was Shane and he looked as intimidating as ever. That last drop of the black stuff hit the bottom of my stomach like a rock as I realised how foolish I'd been and that my dad had not been fluthered. I was looking so hard that he turned my way and our eyes met. I quickly excused myself and dashed to the exit. Being young and fit, once I left the pub, I ran for dear life down through town. I had come to know Sydney, especially the town area, really well and was able to lose him and his two friends. Some of the big departmental stores you can go in off one street and come out on another. I caught a train to North Sydney then took the bus home from there."

"Oh dear, how was that experience for you?" the priest asked, looking quite concerned.

"Terrifying and it was not easy running having downed most of a glass of the black stuff. I could now understand why the Oul Fella was in such a state. Even Ma, once I told her, was now disturbed and in bits, convinced that the Shankill Butchers had come to town."

"Shankill Butchers?" the priest asked.

"A group of thugs who had murdered and maimed many Catholics," Sean continued, after sipping some more tea. "We knew that the oul fella was right and we had to leave Australia; that it would only be a matter of time before they tracked us down. They'd be working overtime to find our home address. While I completed my examinations Da continued to go to work." Sean pulled out his hanky and wiped the tears from his eyes. "One day he didn't return home."

"Your dad? Oh!" exclaimed Father Ted, lost for words.

"They fished him out of Sydney Harbour." Sean wiped his eyes and blew his nose. "And I didn't even get to say goodbye to my own father. The police said that it was too dangerous for us to view his body. Anyhow, better we didn't as he was so badly beaten to a state of being unrecognisable. They think that he may have been thrown off a boat, maybe even the ferry."

Sean wiped his eyes again. "I couldn't even go to my own father's burial."

"That's so sad." Father Ted reached out and patted Sean on the back.

"That must have been so hard for you and your Mum."

Sean gulped some more tea then, recovering, continued. "We left as planned for Auckland."

"You mother, sisters and brothers?" asked Father Ted.

"No, I only had an older sister, Colleen, who was married and living in Perth. They're hardly likely to find her," added Sean. "Perth is like the other side of the world, two thousand miles away from Sydney, and my sister being married had a different surname."

"So, just the two of you?"

Sean took another sip. "Just the two of us."

"Then when did you move to Christchurch?" enquired Father Ted.
Sean pulled out his handkerchief and wiped his eyes again.

"The oul dear got a job in Auckland. We bought a house and settled down in the suburb of Onehunga. Both of us learned to drive and we bought our first car ever. It's just sad that the oul fella never had that opportunity to ever drive a car. He would have liked to but we didn't have any money to speak of. Instead, in Belfast we used bicycles and the bus and none of us could drive. Ma had been a stay at home housewife, like many Irish women at that time. She had no qualifications or marketable skills, so she ended up with a poorly paid cleaning job in Auckland. It helped her to make ends meet and we did own our house. Once again we became settled, enjoying our new surroundings and once again we became complacent, lured into a false sense of security."

"And why not?" interrupted the Father. "They had succeeded in their pointless objective in getting their revenge. You should have had nothing further to worry about."

"We thought so too," replied Sean. "Anyhow, we religiously continued to avoid contact with those in Ireland and kept a low profile just to be sure. I attended Auckland University and completed my degree in 1986. Auckland was an expensive place to live so I remained at home with Ma and together we somehow managed our finances. That was until one day I received a visitor." Sean wiped the tears from his eyes."

"No way, not Shane Gallagher?" suggested Father Ted. "Holy Mother of God, how on earth did he find you?"

"Fortunately not that monster," replied Sean. "But worse. It was the police coming to inform me that my mother had died in a hit and run."

"Oh no, you poor man." Father Ted reached across and stroked Sean's back. "Oh, how dreadful for you after all that had already happened. I'm so sorry for you. It reminds me of Job in the bible. He had so many losses. It was one thing after another but there's always light at the end of a tunnel as Job found out. You've had more than your share of tragedies but unfortunately, accidents do happen. It must have been so hard for you after recently losing your father."

"It was." Sean wiped his eyes. "I didn't know where to turn and I had the job of having to break this news to my sister as well."

"Did they arrest anyone?" enquired Father Ted.

"They call it a cold case as it was unsolved. It wasn't the typical hit and run. The police thought the accident looked suspicious as the damage to her car suggested that somebody had shunted her off the road pushing her into a power pole."

"No! So then you moved to Christchurch?" Father Ted placed his empty cup on the table.

"Yes, given what had happened in Australia and now in Auckland the police advised me that it was best to move away from Auckland. I could have moved back to Australia to somewhere quite distant, like Perth. But that would have put my sister in danger as well."

"So, when was that?" asked the Father.

"Oh, that would have been in 1990, April, I think.

"OK, now I can understand why you're concerned about the van parked across the road. But it's now thirty years that you've lived in Christchurch.

During that time, has anyone tried to kill you?" The Father leaned back on his seat.

"Well, no," replied Sean, "but I've learned to remain vigilant. Every time we've become complacent, another family member has been picked off. It has been a living hell since Northern Ireland."

"Hate is a festering cancer that eats away at the soul," replied Father Ted. "But the victims of your dad's IRA activities would now be at least in their seventies and I'd have thought they would be more concerned over their own health issues rather than chasing somebody on the other side of the world, don't you think?"

"I'd like to think so but it's hard to move on with the thought that there may be someone out there looking to take revenge." Sean put his handkerchief back into his pocket. "And now there's that black van that's sometimes parked across the road. Somebody's watching somebody and maybe waiting for the right moment."

"But you said you had no part in your father's activities and thirty plus years have now passed," replied the Father. "If they were out to get you then why would they waste time on surveillance if they know where you live? I think that if there is someone spying on you then it is for another reason."

"And what reason might that be, Father?" Sean asked. "Could it be my ex-misses? I'd certainly like to get to the bottom of this."

"It could be that but there are several other possibilities." Father Ted cleared his throat and looked out the window, observing Susie in her garden next door. "For instance," he hesitated, "that nosey Chinese neighbour out there. Now how do you know that she's not a Chinese spy? It might even be her and not you who's under surveillance?"

Sean burst out laughing. "That old busy-body? Father, she's just a harmless little old lady. Look at her grey hair! Sure, as you know, on a number of occasions she's done translation work for the Chinese embassy but that doesn't make her a spy. You'd make a good fiction writer, Father."

"Well, I recall you telling me that every time you have been off to the university library to do research she's been keen to come," said the Father.

"Now what's that got to do with being a spy? So she likes books. That might make her a book worm, but not a spy!" Sean laughed again. "She's probably seeking out books written in Mandarin, the University does have a wide selection of books."

"Sorry, what I'm getting at," replied a slightly embarrassed Father, "is that in America the Chinese have infiltrated universities mingling amongst the students and pushing Marxist propaganda. More recently their tactics have been to befriend overseas students from China to gather information on their friends in Hong Kong who are opposed to the Chinese takeover. I understand that it's been pretty bad in Hong Kong with the authorities quick to pounce on those critical of CCP policy. Now your neighbour does seems very defensive of the CCP."

 Sean laughed again. "I have no doubts you're right about China but Russia and the USA all do this type of stuff. Our Susie, I can assure you, is harmless."

"Well, all I'm saying is that it's not necessarily you who's the one under surveillance, Sean. It may even be another neighbour or simply a case of you both getting a little paranoid. I think you need to enjoy the present rather than be imprisoned by the past," said Father Ted.

"I'd like to think so too and after all this time I would hope that the Irish thing is finished but after what I've been through losing both my dad and mum, Father… Maybe I am paranoid."

"Hm, but then," added Father Ted, "I guess you could be on a watch list given your past IRA history, especially if it involved shootings and bombings. In the minds of the authorities you might be considered a dangerous man."

"That was my father," lied Sean. "Oh, though I was actively involved years ago in the protests over the Waihopai American spy station up near Blenheim if that counts for anything. But protests in New Zealand are legal and I took no part in the vandalism. Anyhow, who might be doing the watching and how would they know about these things?"

 "Oh, I guess that the New Zealand secret service and CIA would surely know about everything given all the surveillance tools at their disposal," said the Father.

"Then there are your novels, highly critical of the CIA," added the priest.

"I'm a fiction writer," replied Sean.

"Now then let's look at it from another perspective," suggested the priest.

"We have here a man with a history of violence…

"That was my dad," interrupted Sean.

"… involved in anti-American activities, who on top of this, in his widely read novel, rubbishes the CIA and may even disclose USA secrets."

"If you put it that way it also rubbishes China," replied Sean.

"That's true," agreed Father Ted. "Did Susie read it?"

"She has and keeps asking how I came by all the stuff about China," replied Sean. "She was not at all happy."

"Exactly," said the priest. "She's strongly supportive of the CCP and you haven't known her for that long really."

"Leave my poor Susie alone. She's not a spy, Father. There've been a lot of people coming into my life recently, including you. It's the price of becoming a famous writer," Sean joked.

"So how did you come by all your information?" asked the Father.

"Just pure guess-work, Father, that's all," continued Sean. "I'm a fiction writer not a historian. The CIA and China have better things to do than to go chasing the harmless thousands out there with their conspiracy theories," laughed Sean.

"Hm, well let's just say that if there was some truth to the speculation in your book, then the CIA might also be curious about your source."

"Haha, what source? Like I said, most of it is just conjecture, like the CIA carrying out covert operations in the northern Chinese province of Xinjiang to stir up Uyghur Muslim resistance against their Han overmasters. Though I have to say it's highly likely."

"You do? Why?" The priest looked interested.

"Think about it," explained Sean, "The Turkmenistan–China gas pipe-line supplies much of China's gas through Xinjiang. Disruption of this supply line could be devastating. China already sees the Uyghur Muslim people as a threat and has embarked on a programme of mass genocide and internment camps."

"So sad and in this day and age," commented the priest. "After the Holocaust one might have expected the world to have moved on from human atrocities."

"Stirring up and arming minority groups, funding proxy groups, and using ex-veteran mercenaries for special operations has long been the approach by the CIA," continued Sean. They have a history of overturning regimes in order to gain American control over their oil and other valuable resources. Who do you think is now stealing Syria's oil?"

"Greed is a terrible thing," commented the Father. "Especially when there's no need. God has supplied the world with plenty of resources for everyone to share on this planet. There would be no poverty if we loved our neighbour. But you're mistaken about the CIA. Had they not existed, then there would have been terrorist attacks across the planet."

"Oh, but it's certainly true about the Coronavirus coming out of the Wuhan laboratory," added Sean who was now fired up. "China's wet market explanation is, to put it mildly, pathetic. Everything points to the laboratory."

"I totally agree about China," replied the Father. "What does Susie think about this?"

"Father, leave poor Susie out of it. OK, so she doesn't like China being blamed. She blames America for the virus."

"America? Now that's rather far-fetched," commented the Father. "Holy Mother of God, we all know where the virus originated. The fact is that you do have a history of violence and given that your book is a best-seller and has wide exposure, it's possible that you may be on a watch list," replied Father Ted, "especially if some of what you've said in your book is true. It could suggest a leak within the USA Government or CIA ranks. Sure, I agree that nothing can be proven and one can come up with all sorts of theories. Anything is possible in this day and age. Anyhow, take care and don't let that vehicle across the road trouble you. I must crack on, I have other house calls to make."

57

Chapter Nine

"The world is a stage, but the play is badly cast."

Oscar Wilde

Sergeant first scanned the area to ensure Susie was not in her garden before she briskly walked up the path towards Sean's house. She was keen to pass on the good news to Sean but not Susie.

"Good news Sean," she said as she entered the house.
Sean, who had been sitting in the lounge, finishing a cup of tea, looked up.

"Is there such a thing as good news in this day and age?"

Sergeant laughed, helping herself to one of the comfortable armchairs. "Well," she began. "I've looked up that car plate number on our database. You know the one Susie gave me."

"And how did you get on?" asked Sean.

"I got a security violation," she added.

"A what? What's so good about that and what on Earth is a security violation?" Sean barked. "Are you codding me?"

"Well," replied Sergeant, "It comes up as a security violation when it's something I'm not meant to see."

"Oh, what does that mean?" Sean looked even more perplexed.

"Meaning that whoever was in that car will have nothing to do with Ireland," continued Sergeant. "I'm pretty certain about that."

"So who is it? What's it all about?" asked Sean.

"Hard to say," replied Sergeant. "I know that when there's a police operation, say like to bring down a drug operation, only those involved will have computer access. All other access will be denied. It's all kept hush hush."

"I can assure you that I'm not into drug dealing, but it's a thought," laughed Sean. "A larger cash flow would come in handy as I'm not selling that many books. What do you think I should deal in?"

"Haha, that's just an example," laughed Sergeant. "It could be any activity or it might even involve our secret service, the SIS."

"You mean the people who sit on park benches with a little spy-hole in their newspaper and keep an eye on little old ladies like Susie?" joked Sean.

"Very funny," replied Sergeant. "But it does raise suspicion on the activities of your neighbours."

"Not you too. Leave my little old Susie alone," Sean replied. "It's always the little people who get picked on."

"Interesting conversation," said Father Ted, walking into the room. "It sounds more than small talk," he laughed.

"Where did you come from?" Sergeant looked surprised as she hadn't intended the Father to hear. "Your car wasn't parked out the front."

"He was visiting the jacks" laughed Sean. "Father was driving in the vicinity when he was caught short."

"Telling lies won't get you to heaven," replied a slightly embarrassed priest. "My car is down the road waiting to be serviced. I suspect the battery. It just suddenly died."

"So much for electric cars then if just the ordinary car battery only lasts three to five years," quipped Sean.

"So you suspect Susie?" Father Ted looked interested. "I've always had my suspicions, her embassy connections and all that."

"Not a word to Susie." Sergeant looked sternly at the priest. "It was only intended for Sean's ears."

"And you're telling me this just after I went to the expense of having a security camera installed?" asked Sean. "If I had known it wasn't me being spied on then I wouldn't have bothered."

"Good. I'm pleased that you've had a security camera installed." Sergeant looked surprised. "Finally for once you've taken my advice after how many years?"

 "Both Susie and I had security cameras installed," replied Sean. "They're great, I just have to go to the app on my phone or computer and I can replay all the past action outside the house."

"So who installed them?" Sergeant asked.

"Oh, Susie arranged that through some of her Chinese friends," replied Sean.

 "You let them put an app on your phone and computer," the Father looked worried. "Were you watching them when they were attending to your computer?"

"I was there at the time," replied Sean "And it seems to work really well, Father."

"They could have loaded spyware onto your computer and how do you know what access others may now have to your computer and phone?"

"What do you mean, Father?"

"He means what program, or programs, did they install?" explained Sergeant. "You do have to be careful these days."

"How do I know that? They're the experts," replied Sean. I just fix computers, I'm not into the software side of things."

"And that's the problem," said Sergeant. "Electronics have become so complex we have to put our trust in others. It pays to use a reputable company."

"I thought as much. Susie might be a Chinese agent." Father Ted looked worried.

"Not necessarily," replied Sergeant. "The violation could have been for a number of reasons. It's not just about safeguarding operations. We have a lot of personal information about people; some who are dangerous and on our watch list. We sometimes are alerted if their car drives past. Since they deinstitutionalised mental hospital patients there are a lot of nutters out there in the community."

"Information on citizens? Goodness gracious, Big Brother in little New Zealand?" Father Ted looked shocked.

"It's far, far worse overseas Father," said Sean. They use cameras for facial recognition and have street cameras everywhere; probably even hack into private security cameras like mine. In China there is one camera for every two citizens. They have cameras everywhere spying on the population."

"My goodness!" exclaimed Father Ted. "They must have a large percentage of the country sitting behind screens observing everyone else then."

"No need; the cameras interact with computer algorithms designed to identify certain people and certain offending…"

"Like what, Sean?" asked Father Ted.

"Like people not wearing Covid masks, people not isolating, people discarding litter on the street; you know, anything really important," Sean smirked.

"What! Petty crimes, for goodness sake what is the world coming to? Then what, capital punishment?" Father Ted looked interested.

"Then they forward the footage to the appropriate people policing that particular behaviour," replied Sean "and the perpetrators might be arrested."

"And have to do twenty press-ups," joked Sergeant. "Look, I'm not agreeing with Ted but how do you know that your camera isn't being used as surveillance on yourself?" Sergeant seemed concerned. "Do you know exactly who Susie got to install it and where the cameras came from? Now I'm in no way suggesting some Chinese conspiracy theory, Ted. I'm just not going to be drawn into going there. Unlike you and Sean I'm not going to be drawn into conspiracy theories."

"Well, from what I understand there are Chinese agents everywhere, especially in universities throughout the world where they're trying to convert students to Marxism," said Father Ted. "That is fact." The Father now looked more serious.

"Susie is not a spy," repeated Sean.

"Just be very careful," warned the Father. "Anyhow, before Sergeant arrived I was starting to tell you about this Irishman at mass. I almost mistook him for you as the two of you look so much alike. He asked me about you."

"And you had better have told him nothing," reminded Sergeant.

"Of course not." The priest looked indignant. "In my profession confidentiality is paramount, otherwise our parishioners wouldn't confess. This man is from Belfast and said he recognised you but the person he named was Sean O'Malley who he said was his cousin. But he must have got it wrong as you are Sean O'Brien."

"What's his name?" asked an anxious Sean.

"Patrick Fitzgerald," replied the Father.

"Paddy Fitzgerald, you say? Is he about my age?"

"He is," replied the Father.

"My cousin here, living in Christchurch, nineteen thousand kilometres away from Ireland? Now that's unbelievable. What a small world. I've got to meet him."

"No, you don't! Don't be foolish Sean, just remember what happened to other family members when their cover was blown," reminded Sergeant.

"But this is my cousin, my best friend, Sergeant. Look, that was thirty years ago when my mother was killed. All these years plus I've suffered being away from friends and extended family. I never even got to see my own father buried. Paddy was my best friend and will surely keep my whereabouts secret. I'm sure, Father Ted here will hold him to that won't you?"

"I will," replied the Father.

"Can you arrange a meeting, Father?"

"I can indeed, Sean. Better is a dish of vegetables where love is than a fattened ox served with hatred."

"Meaning what, Father?"

"It's from the book of Proverbs. The greatest gift that one can give is love. It is not healthy to be separated from people you love," replied the Father.

"You've been warned," scolded Sergeant as she stormed out of the room. There was not much she could do to protect Sean from the fate of his parents once his cover was blown.

Chapter Ten

"We have always found the Irish a bit odd. They refuse to be English."
Winston Churchill

Sean eagerly peered out the window at the priest's car parked outside his house. He watched as the Father and a stranger from the past left the car and walked up the path. Yes, it was certainly Paddy but a somewhat older version, grey and balding. It had been over forty years since he had last seen his cousin. I guess we have all aged, he thought as he touched the balding area on the back of his head. He too no longer had that thick crop of beautiful brown springy hair. Sean left his observation post and sprinted to the door to welcome a long lost friend.

"Paddy, wow! How great it is to see you." Sean gave him a huge hug. "I can't wait to hear about all our family in Ireland. I've missed them so much."

Paddy looked at Sean. "I'm really so glad to see you too and know that you're alive and well. It's been hard for all of us. And your parents and sister?"

"I'll tell you about them later. Please take a seat," he instructed, directing the Father and Paddy to the couch.

"No, you sit down, Sean," offered the Father. "I'll fetch the tea. You two have a lot to catch up on."

"Yes, a cup of tea would be good," said Paddy as he settled into a seat. "Those days in Ireland as children were so hard. No money and the constant worry of the landlord knocking at the door but still we never went without our cup of tea, even if it was more to soothe our nerves and help us through another day. Those were indeed troubling times."

"It was brutal," agreed Sean "and we're so lucky to be fit and alive."

"If you'd asked me how I'd like my cup of tea, Father, then I'd have replied in a cup," joked Paddy, "but anyhow milk but no sugar will suit me just fine."

"Good to see you've still got your wicked sense of humour," laughed Sean.

"Sean," Paddy looked at him somewhat seriously. "It was such a shock to us all when one day your family just disappeared never to be heard of again. We didn't know what to think, whether you were alive, incarcerated or what. Da in particular was so upset worrying about his sister."

"They were very close," said Sean. "They were a close knit family."

"When you didn't come home that night of the bombing your mum and sister came around." continued Paddy. "Your mum she was in bits, a wreck not knowing if you were alive or dead. Da wasn't at all surprised though when your mum found out that Uncle Danny had been caught red-handed. He'd often said your dad was playing with fire and would one day get burnt. But why he never went to prison, remains troubling to us and a mystery to this day. We all knew what he and you were up to in that back room, making bombs."

"Oh dear!" exclaimed Father Ted from the kitchen, shaking his head and looking over at Sean. "That's not at all what you told me Sean."

"My dad was a war hero," replied a proud Sean. "It would have been embarrassing for the authorities to put him on trial when they were trying to convince the Irish public and the British that the rioting, bombings and shooting were just a group of militant extremists. Even worse would have been to send a bomb-maker to prison where he could train others in the skill."

"Now that does make a lot of sense and is of great relief because we'd heard rumours he'd turned traitor and done some deal," replied Paddy. "At the time a lot of IRA leaders were arrested, suggesting that the rumour might be true. We felt gutted that you'd leave poor Liam O'Mahony to take the rap."

"We didn't know. We were put in different cells and never saw Liam again. They told us nothing. We were simply pawns in a game of cat and mouse," replied Sean.

"Liam was livid and swore he took no part," added Paddy. "He said he'd been set up; that no sooner had the bomb gone off than the police were there to arrest him. And his family, those poor people, Holy Mary, they went through hell. Didn't have a kind word to say about you or your dad. They could have murdered you there and then. We all could have after what you put us all through."

"Oh, Liam certainly played a part, I can assure you," replied Sean "and we too believed we'd been set up. No sooner had we reached our car than the Garda was onto us. Have you ever known the Garda to be that quick off the mark?"

"Does indeed sound like a set-up to me," sighed Paddy. "I wish we'd known then because as family we bore the guilt and shame and didn't speak of you kindly to others."

"Then there were all those poor people at the pub who were killed and injured," added Paddy. "It was so sad to hear the court testimonies of the injuries received and how so many innocent lives and dreams had been destroyed."

"We were at war," replied Sean. "It was a civil war between the Irish and the British. In war there are always casualties. We couldn't just stand by and be picked off by those murderous thugs."

"You have no remorse for even innocent lives lost?" questioned Father Ted from the kitchen.

"In war, civilians often fall victim, Father," said Sean. "When Da dropped bombs on German cities it was not just on military targets and he had the British government's full blessing."

"So how is Uncle Danny, Aunt Deidre and your sister?" enquired Paddy. "Are they living in Christchurch?"

"We also went through very hard times," replied Sean wiping away the tears in his eyes with his hand. "We took refuge in Australia but that didn't stop the Shankill Butchers."

"A brutal bunch," interrupted Paddy. "Though the bombing did some damage and in a small way we were grateful."

"Despite cutting off all contact with family and friends ..." Sean paused to produce a handkerchief. "They finally succeeded in killing my dad. Fished him out of Sydney harbour." Sean wiped his eyes with his handkerchief. The Father, who had just entered the room with cups of tea, quickly reached across and patted him softly on the back. Sean gave his nose a good blow.

"Oh dear, I'm so sorry," said Paddy, wiping his eyes then picking up his cup of tea and waiting for Sean to recover. "How dreadful. Then you left and came to New Zealand?"

"Just me and Ma. My sister got married and stayed in Australia."

"She was a bit older than us and like a second mother. Many a time she saved our necks as wild young boyos from getting into trouble. I liked her a lot and really missed her. I remember when we used to help ourselves to some of the black stuff from Uncle Danny's beer mug when he slipped out to the jacks or had nodded off half pissed," Paddy laughed.

"But even then he still noticed the tide had gone out," chuckled Sean. "He didn't miss much. We had a lot of fun in those days."

"Is Aunty here in Christchurch too then? asked Paddy. "I'd like to catch up with her."

Sean wiped his eyes again. "They got her as well."

"Sorry?" Paddy looked shocked. "They got her? Oh, Da would have been gutted had he known. He was never the same again when you all disappeared. Life was never the same for any of us."

"Well, I think it was them. She died in a suspicious car accident in Auckland not long after."

"Oh, now I see why Father Ted told me that I needed to keep all this secret but surely the danger has long since passed."

"Exactly my thoughts," said the Father.

"They were a vindictive lot," continued Paddy, "but all of this happened a long time ago." Paddy took a sip of tea then continued. "Wasn't easy for us in Ireland either. After the bombing our family had to avoid Protestant areas. As you know the Shankill Butchers had a reputation and we were all likely targets. Da had warned Uncle Danny that no good would come from joining the IRA but your dad could be quite stubborn. He just wouldn't listen. He never did; he was a man on a mission. So sad but the war probably made him like that. Like so many others he got dragged into the IRA because he was so angry at being treated like a second-rate citizen, especially after he'd put his life on the line during the Second World War fighting for a better world. But the Shankill Road bombing made everything worse for us."

"It had to be done," replied Sean. "They had to be stopped from injuring and killing Catholics. The Garda sat by and did nothing."

"I know, and we had no choice either after the bombing," continued Paddy. "Da had to join the IRA to get protection from Protestant retribution. As I understand it, there was a lot of coercion going on in both Catholic and Protestant camps; people being forced into the conflict. Da had never wanted a part but reluctantly agreed to do some small jobs for the IRA. Well, like your dad, his luck also ran out and he was caught by the Garda. They imprisoned him at the Maze for several months."

"That's where Liam was imprisoned," said Sean.

"Oh yes, Liam, poor Liam. So brutal. My dad said the man was in bits; had a terrible time in prison; ended up badly beaten, a bad dose on several occasions. On one occasion he was close to death. And his family had a terrible time having to change houses to keep one move ahead of the Shankill Butchers. The IRA didn't want to know them after the bombing as Liam had served his purpose. In the end, the family exhausted all options and left Ireland for a life somewhere overseas. Just like you, one day they simply disappeared. Gone! Address unknown. I guess it had to be that way. As for Liam, he developed severe depression in prison, and it's uncertain whether he died from poor health or whether he took his own life shortly after leaving."

"And your dad and mum and my cousins, how are they?" asked Sean.

"Still in Belfast but Da and Ma have since died. After the bombing my dad's life was a mess especially after being drawn into the IRA and having done time. With a criminal record he found it hard to get any job and they couldn't travel overseas. It was hard for our family and even harder for Ma and Da. Perhaps best they did die without learning what happened to your parents. Da, he'd have been devastated to learn his sister was murdered. We all spent many days, years even, of anxiety pondering over your whereabouts and wellbeing," added Paddy. "But Da was right, nothing good comes from violence."

"A wise man," said Father Ted. "Do not be envious of evil men, nor desire to be with them. For their heart devises violence and their lips speak of troublemaking."

"Sorry?" replied Paddy.

"From Proverbs," replied the Father. "I trust your dad sought forgiveness for his part?"

"Most certainly, Father. Many times he went to confession and knelt before the Virgin Mary. Yes, he was also angry at how Catholics were being treated but he opposed using violence. But Sean, you'll be pleased that most of the Shankill Butchers gang were finally caught in 1979 and spent many years in prison for their horrendous crimes."

"About time," replied Sean. "How many people had to die before justice was done? They were quick to put Catholics in prison."

"May I ask what crimes?" asked Father Ted.

"Kidnapping, beating, knifing and torturing Catholics as well as over twenty-three murders."

"Dear me, how terrible," gasped Father Ted

"They were such an evil bunch," continued Paddy, "and, dare I say it but, part of me was glad about the Shankill Pub bombing. It was justice served. Unfortunately their leader managed to avoid a long prison sentence but he got his just deserts in 1980s when he was shot in the head many times by IRA hit men. There's talk in Ireland that the IRA were assisted by loyalists who wanted him gone, which could very well be true. Anyway Sean, you needn't worry further about them hunting you down as most of them are now dead and gone."

"And that's what I've been telling Sean," said the Father. "You should confess your sins and move on with life. You can't change the past."

"I wouldn't want to. It was the right thing to do," replied Sean.

"Oh, but there was the case of Bobby Bates, one of the sergeants," said Paddy. "He was shot dead in the 1990s by the son of a UDA man who he had killed. I guess revenge always finds a way of raising its ugly head, sometimes through the next generation who experienced the loss of a father or mother."

Paddy put down his empty cup. "But not that I'm saying that would happen to you, Sean."

"Hatred is a terrible sin and can be generational. Revenge leads to revenge as violence leads to more violence. The only answer is forgiveness," added Father Ted. "I thought that Bates had sought forgiveness and had become a Christian before coming out of prison."

"I wouldn't know," replied Paddy. "Often it's just a ploy to get probation."

"Maybe," replied the Father, "but it's not for us to judge."

"Did you hear what happened to Shane Gallagher, to Knuckles?" asked Sean.

"That nasty piece! Not at all, thank goodness. He was one to keep well clear of. His two sons have also developed reputations and one is red-headed and looks exactly like Shane. Why do you ask?"

"Da was chased by him in Sydney and shortly after they found dad's body in Sydney harbour. It sounded like one of his jobs, since the police said Da was beaten unrecognisable."

"You didn't see the body then, Sean?" asked Paddy.

"No, the police advised us that if we turned up for a viewing or the funeral we could be next," replied Sean.

"Then how can you be sure that Uncle Danny is dead?" asked Paddy.

"Now that's a very good point," said Father Ted.

"Well, he's never been seen since," replied Sean.

"Your dad was a war hero. It wouldn't be unlike him to do a noble act by disappearing to save your skins."

"A nice thought, Paddy, but if he did then it didn't work for Ma, she was still killed and after all this time he's never resurfaced." Sean gathered the empty cups.

"A car accident, and an unproven homicide," said Father Ted. "Paddy does have a valid point, though I would have thought your dad, if alive, might have returned in later years especially after most of the gang were incarcerated."

"Would he have known?" asked Paddy.

"Oh, undoubtedly if he was alive. He kept up with Irish news," Sean replied.

"Then I'm sorry but sadly he must be dead then," concluded the priest.

"So what brought you to New Zealand of all places Paddy?" asked Sean. "Why Christchurch when there are a million places on this planet?"

"It's unbelievable, I had a dream. The Virgin Mary told me that my wife and I needed to start a new life in Christchurch, New Zealand," replied Paddy.

"And now you can see why," confirmed Father Ted.

"Dreams are just that," laughed Sean. "There's nothing in them."

"Well," said Father Ted, "after Saint Patrick was captured in England as a young lad he was sold into slavery in Ireland. One day he had a dream that he must escape and he'd find a boat in a certain place where he would get a passage back to England. He did just that and found the boat exactly where he was told in the dream it would be. With the Virgin Mary helping at the helm he was able to make a safe passage back across those turbulent waters of the Irish Sea."

"Is that true or just blarney?" asked Sean.

"True," replied the Father.

"So, why Christchurch?" asked Sean.

"I don't know but the dream made sense. Shortly after there was the Christchurch earthquake and a big demand for tradesmen to rebuild the city. It was an opportunity for a better life and was too hard to turn down."

"Is it still bad in Northern Ireland?" asked Sean.

"It's improving," replied Paddy. "Since you left there have been ceasefires, peace talks and improved conditions for Catholics. The IRA effectively disbanded but there are always those who have unfinished scores and those who want to break away from the UK. Change takes time and some people are never satisfied. The IRA political party Sinn Féin is now the most popular party and reunification of the north with Ireland seems likely in the future.

"So you're saying that there's no more bombings or shootings?" asked Father Ted.

"Most of the time none at all," replied Paddy. "Things have changed for the better. The old divisions are disappearing but there is still distrust if the government elected is largely Unionist. The Good Friday Agreement involving power sharing was a major break-through and both groups, as a consequence, disarmed."

"Or stock-piled and reorganised in preparation for the next conflict," smirked Sean, with Father Ted looking on disapprovingly. "Well, we all know Father, that in the past, cease fires have just been perceived as opportunities by both sides to regroup and get the upper hand."

"So there's finally peace after all these years?" asked a hopeful Father.

"I wouldn't say that," replied Paddy. "The loyalists still want to remain attached to the United Kingdom and the republicans want to break away. Nothing has changed so power sharing seems to be the only solution."

"Then it could very well return to another war?" suggested Sean.

"It could." continued Paddy. "Sinn Féin has been pushing for the revival of our Irish culture, which has not gone down well with the loyalists."

"And so they should," replied Sean. "The English have a history of assimilation. Everything must always be the English way."

"Agreed," replied Paddy. "But they're pushing for the revival of the Irish language when now only six percent, if that, can speak it. Seriously, is there any point reviving a second language, in this day and age, when English is the language understood throughout the world?"

"Bollocks! It's a part of our culture," replied Sean. "It's who we are."

"Maybe, but it's more a case of Sinn Féin weaponising language in order to rid Northern Ireland of its British ties, whereas the Catholic—Protestant thing is not now such a big issue. Restoring a language spoken by less than half of the population only serves to divide us further to the extent we will never be one people." Paddy looked concerned.

 "Ha, well the Irish language had its uses back when I was in Ireland," laughed Sean. "I remember Da saying that incarcerated IRA members used it to communicate so the prison guards wouldn't know what they were saying."

"And these days it's not uncommon for Protestants and Catholics to marry. My big sister even married a Protestant," continued Paddy.

"She didn't?" replied a shocked Sean. "How could she marry one of them?"

"And," replied Paddy, "her father-in-law was a member of the UVF, but her husband isn't at all political. Things are certainly changing for the better."

"What!" Sean looked shocked. "Marrying a loyalist?"

"We're going to have to go," said Father Ted looking at his watch and noting Sean was getting agitated.

"Can we catch up soon?" asked Sean who was still quite shocked and shaken.

"Most definitely," replied Paddy. "Meeting you and knowing you're alive and kicking has been a great weight off my mind. If only my parents had known."

"Oh, I forgot to ask what you do for a job?" asked Paddy

"I have my own business of fixing computers. Unfortunately writing books doesn't pay the bills," added Sean.

"You write?" Paddy asked.

"Here's a complimentary copy of my latest book," said Sean, passing Paddy a copy. "I hope you enjoy it."

"I'm sure I'll find the book a good read," said Paddy, rising from the sofa.

Chapter Eleven

"The strongest of all warriors are these two - time and patience."

Leo Tolstoy

It was a cold winter's afternoon when Sean next met with Paddy. Sean observed him coming up the concrete pathway which was wet from the rain the night before. Father Ted, like Sergeant, didn't knock, he just bowled into the house with Paddy.

"So this is the misses, a policewoman?" asked Paddy, looking over towards Sergeant.

"No we're just friends," replied Sergeant, looking a little embarrassed. "You could say I'm his minder if you want to put it that way."

"Ah! Police protection?" suggested Paddy. "What? Here in peaceful New Zealand?"

"Well, we have to be very careful given Sean's history," replied Sergeant. "He's already lost two family members and we're not overly keen on him re-establishing Irish connections."

"Sorry Paddy, I should have introduced you, this is Sergeant. She is a police sergeant but Sergeant is also her name."

"This is your cousin?" enquired Sergeant.

Paddy smiled. "Yes, I've been that since the day I was born but one day he and his family just simply disappeared off this planet. Holy Mother of God, it was so terrible to suddenly lose my best friend, then to go through a period of grieving, believing they'd all been killed by that brutal gang of thugs as well as the trauma of believing we might be next. Those were troubling times, dire enough without all of this other stuff happening as well."

"Troubling times? Other stuff?" Sergeant questioned.

"That's right: shootings, riots, bombings, it was horrible, not a time I'd wish to revisit," replied Paddy.

"And not a time we would wish upon Sean now," added Sergeant.

"Sergeant is Māori —you know the indigenous people of New Zealand," said Sean, taking the opportunity to move the conversation to safer grounds. "Her line comes from a famous Māori chief called Hone Heke."

"Hone? What a funny name." Paddy looked amused.

"Hone Heke, was the feller who cut down the flagpole that bore the British flag at Waitangi. That was where the treaty between the British Crown and Māori was signed," informed Sean. "Now Hone is my type of feller who stood up for his rights. He fought till the bitter end. Isn't that right Sergeant?"

"Kaua e mate wheke mate ururoa", replied Sergeant.

"Meaning?" asked Sean.

"Don't die like an octopus, die like a hammerhead shark. It's a Māori saying," said Sergeant.

"Can you explain it more?" asked the priest.

"The shark fights to the bitter end, whereas the octopus gives up."

"In other words what Sergeant is saying is that when it's got to be done it's got to be done. No fluffing around. Procrastination never won any wars," added Sean.

"Never started any either," laughed Paddy.

"Something Irish about that," joked Sergeant. "But yes, I'm related to Hone Heke and proud of it. He was a great rangatira."

"There's no place for violence," chided Father Ted. "It takes time and patience, Sean. Change doesn't just happen overnight and Sergeant if you're related to Hone Heke then you may be Irish."

"Irish, I doubt it! Don't be silly. What do you mean?" Sergeant looked puzzled.

"Well, in the nineteenth century a newspaper article in Ireland claimed that Hone Heke was Irish and was born in Tipperary."

"Total rubbish," barked Sergeant. "A load of garbage."

"His name was Hickey," continued the priest, "and he became a New Zealand inhabitant after his ship was wrecked off New Zealand. He married the local chief's daughter," continued the priest.

"Are you serious?" Sean looked at him with disbelief, "or just codding us?"

"It's rubbish, Sean. Can't you see that Ted's just trying to wind me up?" Sergeant did not look happy.

"Definitely true about the article but of course, you're right Sergeant, it's a load of rubbish. Even then newspapers printed fake news, but some people in Ireland believed it and may do so to this day," laughed the priest. "The Irish saw Hone Heke as a hero."

"Then why did he cut down the flagpole?" asked Paddy. "Did he have something against flags?"

"You mean flagpoles?" joked Sean. "He cut it down four times."

"Four times, now that's rather extreme. I've heard of enraged people burning flags like in Derry, when hundreds gathered and applauded a bonfire involving the burning of union jacks. But tell me was it because he was opposed to the treaty?" Paddy looked puzzled.

"Not at all," said Father Ted. "In fact he was the first Maori chief to sign. He was the leader of a North Island tribe, the ah…"

"Ngapuhi," said Sergeant.

"That's the one," he continued. "He was a very intelligent man who feared the French and rum sellers taking over. He had the foresight to see the benefits of being part of the British Empire, the world superpower at that time, and expected the Māori to benefit immensely through fairer trade with the European. Oh, and he was also involved in the compilation of the first Māori dictionary and maybe even the translation of the treaty into Māori. He was a Christian I believe."

"He cut it down Paddy, because of unfulfilled promises made by the British," explained Sergeant. "It's that simple, the English broke the treaty time and time again and they wonder why even today Māori are unhappy. They just bulldozed their way into New Zealand and expected Māori to drop everything: their language, customs and to conform to their ways, just the same as the English in Ireland."

"Indeed, just like Ireland," barked Sean.

"Undoubtedly there were injustices," added the Father. "And on one hand it's easy for the Māori to take all the benefits of British citizenship and its advanced technology, yet on the other, it takes time, especially for a Māori Chief seeing his power being eroded away and relinquished to the crown. And it's really no different to the change needed in Northern Ireland; it all takes time but there's no place for violence."

"Interesting," replied Paddy. "It seems that every country has its own history of colonisation, exploitation and assimilation, leaving behind a lot of bad feelings. For me, I'm past bickering over Northern Ireland issues. I'm sick and tired of them and, at this time in my life, more than content with a weekly game of golf and a Guinness or two."

"Do you take two spare pairs of socks to golf, Paddy?" asked Sean.

"Now why would I do that?" asked Paddy.

"Just in case you get a hole in one," laughed Sean. "Seriously, Sergeant and I have so much in common," Sean said as he sat down on the sofa.

"Sorry, you have a lot in common?" Paddy looked puzzled. "Father's already explained that she's not really Irish."

"No, I mean being colonised by the English, Paddy," clarified Sean. "And the Māori like those of us in Northern Ireland had our land stolen right from under our noses by the English."

"And it led to the Māori wars in our case," added Sergeant. "Land ownership is important to our people and the English didn't understand that or respect our culture. It was all one big land grab."

"Oh yes, history is like a worn out gramophone with greed raising its ugly head time and time again across the world but may I ask what makes you think Northern Ireland is your land, Sean?" asked the Father.

"Well, we occupied it before England," replied Sean.

"And who's we? may I ask? From my history lessons at school," continued Father Ted, "Ireland's been occupied many times before and as Irish we are descendants from Celts, Pics, Normans and Vikings…"

"And Romans?" Sergeant suggested.

"Surprisingly not, Sergeant. They never reached Ireland, not to say they weren't interested," said Father Ted. "In fact they think the earliest known people were from the Black Sea area and Middle East. If anyone can call it their land, it is them. Civilisation migrated initially from Mesopotamia so in reality we're all migrants. What right do any of us have to claim land as our own?"

"We don't have that problem in New Zealand. Māori are the Tangata Whenua," laughed Sergeant, trying to wind Sean up.

"And what's that?" asked Paddy.

"The people of the land," replied Sergeant. "We are the people of the land but originally they say we migrated from Taiwan. Apparently we're related to the Taiwanese inhabitants of five thousand years ago."

"Then next time you see Susie you can tell her that Taiwan is not a province of China, that it belongs to the Māori," joked Sean. "I'd love to see her face when you tell her. Haha."

"So would I," said Father Ted. "Taiwan never was their province, it has its own indigenous people and over its history has at times been occupied by both China and Japan. Dare I say it but Taiwan is an independent country. But Sergeant, I'm sorry to inform you but you were not the first inhabitants in New Zealand."

"Ah, now you're talking about the Moriori?" suggested Sergeant.

"Much earlier than that. I'm talking back in the Neolithic Bronze Age and I'm afraid that this time Sean might really have the last laugh," grinned the priest.

"I find that hard to believe," scoffed Sergeant.

"Tell me more?" demanded Sean, smirking at Sergeant. "Please do."

"Well, I understand there's evidence in the Coromandel, Auckland and elsewhere of those early Celts who settled in Ireland also settling in New Zealand," explained the priest.

"The Irish were here first? Did you hear that Sergeant?" laughed Sean. "Father, you're wonderful, you've made my day. Haha."

"I don't believe it. Seriously, how would they get here that long ago? Ireland's on the other side of the world," said Sergeant. "It's not possible."

"Well, experts have found ancient standing boulders— some with writing, similar to those found in Ireland. They were placed with precision for purposes like navigation," explained the priest.

"So where are these people now?" asked Paddy. "I've not long been in New Zealand but I understood that when the first Europeans arrived there were only Māori and a small number of Moriori."

"Irish stew," laughed Sergeant, trying to get her own back on Sean. "Very tasty." She licked her lips.

"Then there were red-headed fair skinned people who lived in Turehu before the Maori. In fact the Maori refer to them in their culture."

"True, the Patupaiarehe, but in our legend they were a mythical fairy-like people who lived in the mountains and forests," said Sergeant.

"Leprechauns," laughed Sean. "You also had Leprechauns? Now that's very funny."

"Ah, but it turns out that they weren't mythical," replied the priest. "There is a lot of evidence including stone buildings and wooden artefacts that have been discovered. They most definitely existed."

"Red-headed, did you say?" Paddy looked surprised. "They had to have been Irish."

"That's right," laughed Sean. "Red hair genetically, has Irish and Scottish origin."

"Sean," said Paddy, changing the subject. "I read your book and enjoyed it immensely. "You're a true Irishman and say what you think. You call a spade a spade."

"Don't encourage him," cautioned Father Ted. "Sometimes it is better to remain silent than upset the wrong people."

"Thank you, Paddy," replied Sean. "None of this politically correct stuff so somebody won't be offended. I hope you will give it a review. Writers welcome honest feedback. A five star would be very nice!"

Paddy hesitated and looked towards Sean anxiously. "It was so good, I just had to tell my sister in Ireland about it. She wants to come to New Zealand and visit you."

"I warned you," growled Sergeant looking at Sean. "Didn't I tell you this would come to no good?"

"Sorry, I know about the need for all this secrecy but she latched onto who you were when she saw your picture at the back of the book. She recognised you straight away; the spitting image of your dad. But she already knew that you were here."

"How could she? I trusted you," Sean replied in disbelief. "Sure I'd love to see her but at the same time I wouldn't welcome a bullet. I can't see how she'd know I was in New Zealand. I've told no one."

"Calm down, Sean, it's time to move on," said Father Ted, patting him on the back. "Family is important. Surely you don't want to end up going to your grave without first catching up with all your relatives? What's the point of life if you're going to continue to live in a bubble, constantly fearing that someone out there wants you dead?"

"It happened to my mum and dad but maybe you're right, Father. It's been hell for us living in fear, ostracised from friends and family all these years," said Sean.

"Is that a yes?" asked a hopeful Paddy.

"No it isn't," interrupted Sergeant, "and he's not living in a bubble. He has a life. In fact he's more sociable than a lot of people I visit in the community."

"A maybe," replied Sean. "I'm going to have to think about it."

"There's nothing to think about," said Sergeant. "It's too dangerous. Just remember what happened to other family members."

"Any children?" asked Paddy, conveniently changing the subject.

"I didn't want them because I feared for their safety given the circumstances," replied Sean. "The misses wanted children so when I wouldn't agree, she left me."

"Did she know about Ireland?" asked Paddy.

"Hell, I wasn't telling her that," said Sean. "She might never have married me otherwise."

"Now I realise how hard it must have been for you too. It was so hard for all of us," replied Paddy. "If only your dad had listened to good advice. My dad may not have been a war hero but he had a wise head on his shoulders."

Father Ted rose from the sofa. "Well, best be off."

They agreed to meet again before Father Ted and Paddy left the house, leaving Sean to reflect on the meeting and to face Sergeant's wrath.

Chapter Twelve

"Above all, keep fervent in your love for one another, because love covers a multitude of sins." (1 Peter 4:8)

It was now two weeks since Sean and Paddy had met. Sean was somewhat ambivalent in respect to meeting Paddy's sister. Yes, Father Ted was right, family was important and he'd regretted having had to leave Ireland without ever seeing his grandmother, uncles and aunties and cousins again. On the other hand, thirty plus years had passed and they'd grown apart. He could hardly believe that one of his cousins had married a Protestant, of all things, one linked to the Ulster Volunteer Force. Sergeant's warnings could not be ignored, reconnecting with family could prove a fatal error. Of more concern was how his cousin already knew that he was in New Zealand. Who else knew?

Sean was deep in thought when there was a loud knock at the door; a chilling reminder of that day that he had opened it to learn of his mother's death. His only visitors ever were Sergeant and Father Ted and they knew just to enter unannounced. There could be a bullet waiting for him on the other side of the door. He froze for a second in trepidation, staring blankly towards the door. Was this how his life was to end? He quickly snapped out of his trance, approached the door and secured the lock. With the door now secure, he apprehensively edged closer to peer through the peephole. Standing outside was a tall elderly man and a short grey-headed woman, both who looked innocuous enough. It now seemed safe for him to slide back the lock and cautiously edge the door open. He stood there, frozen in disbelief.

"Well, aren't you going to invite us in?" asked the unshaven man in a strong Australian accent. Sean was somewhat frightened by his bellicosity. "Bloody cold standing out here!"

Sean stood flabbergasted. "Colleen, is that you?"

"Of course it is, Silly. Surely you recognise your own sister?"

An overwrought Sean, in tears, threw himself forward, firmly embracing his sister tightly then returned with some reservation to hug Trev. Trev wouldn't have a bar of it though as he stepped back.

"Na mate, hugging's for sheilas," he said as he extended his right hand, giving a firm handshake.

"Colleen, Trev, what on earth are you doing here?" Sean was overjoyed, wiping the tears from his eyes. "How did you find me?"

"Are you going to let us in? If we stand out here any longer we'll turn into ice-blocks," complained Trev.

"Of course, come in. Do you need somewhere to stay?"

"Do we ever? Took you a long time to ask." Trevor dragged a large suitcase into view that he'd hidden behind a small shrub and they quickly moved inside. "Thought you'd never ask mate, but it's bloody cold in here too," he added, shaking. "What are you, an Eskimo?"

"It's been such a long time," said Colleen who was also tearful.

"Thirty odd years, but we have kept in touch over emails," replied Sean. "You weren't followed, I hope?"

"It's just not the same as meeting someone in the flesh," Colleen responded. "I've longed for this day. My, but how you've changed from the young skinny brother I remember. I might be six years older but nowhere near as grey."

"Nor as fat," added Trev, rubbing his hands and trying to get warm. "Where's your heater?"

Sean went into the lounge and switched on the heat pump before returning.

"What happened to that nice brown springy hair and you've got wrinkles?" Colleen stopped the tears from rolling down her face.

"It's called getting old," said Sean, feeling his age. "I guess I turned grey early with all the worries after Da was murdered."

"So sad," Colleen said, pulling out a handkerchief and wiping her eyes. "I got such a shock the day that Ma rang with the news about Da. I thought we'd be safe in Australia."

"I was so paranoid at the time that I insisted she ring from a public phone box," Sean said. "You weren't followed?" Sean looked worried and peered out the lounge window.

"We're very careful after all that's happened," replied Colleen. "When Ma died it was a reminder to me that my life was also endangered. But fortunately in Perth we're safe and well away from everything."

"Ha, from everything? You've gotta be kidding, Cole. Ha, wasn't for long, not after Pine Gap," taunted Trev. "It's not the Irish we have to watch these days, it's Big Brother who's not at all happy."

"That's right," said Colleen, who took the matter more seriously. "For a while we had a black van parked across the road nearly every day," "Our oldest son, just like Da — a wiz at electronics, said they could be out there monitoring our every activity and had probably hacked into our computer."

"Really?" Sean looked surprised. "Who are they?"

"Don't give me that bullshit, you know very well who, mate," said Trev. "Remember nine eleven?"

"Is the Pope a Catholic?" laughed Sean.

"Al-Qaeda tried it on again in 2006," continued Trev. "Would you believe it, liquid explosives in bottles intended to blow up planes heading for the States from London. MI6 and the UK police discovered the plot."

"Sorry, but what's all this got to do with the black van?" asked Sean.

"A hell of a lot, mate," replied Trev. "It's how they discovered the plot. They can make cameras so small these days you'd never know they're there mate. The occupants of the house had no idea they were on camera."

"Then Big Brother could be listening into our conversation right now," suggested Sean. "There's been a black van parked across the road on and off for the last month or so."

"Holy Mother of God!" Colleen looked shocked. "You too?"

"Ha, be warned then," laughed Trev. "I'm not at all surprised. You're a dangerous man. Did ya hear that?" Trev shouted at the wall. "He's a dangerous man."

"So what work are you doing now, Trev?" asked Sean.

"Working down in the mines. Plenty of mining jobs in Oz, mate and good money if you're prepared to get your hands dirty," added Trev. "Australia's the lucky country. Plenty of bucks to be made."

"You enjoy that sort of work, Trev? Like it's pretty physical at your age."

"Better than a kick up the backside, mate. I get to bring home the bacon and the misses here cooks it up. Soon we'll be taking the pension though."

Sean walked ahead towards the hallway. "I'll show you to your room. Quite small but I live on my own." Sean led them down the hallway to a room not much bigger than the double bed in it. "I'll have to get you some sheets as the bed isn't made up."

"Just leave me the sheets and blankets and I can do the rest," offered Colleen. "Sorry, we should have warned you we were coming but these days we don't know if our place is bugged."

"Course there's bugs? There's those bloody cockroaches crawling up and down our walls," joked Trev. "Plenty of bugs in Australia. If the CIA don't get ya then the poisonous snakes or bugs will."

"You've gotta die of something," laughed Colleen as they carried their bags to the bedroom.

"Cole, did you check the luggage for snakes before we left?" asked Trev.

"Snakes?" Sean looked worried.

"He's just codding you," laughed Colleen. "It's his Aussie sense of humour."

Colleen and Trev returned about twenty minutes later to join Sean in the lounge.

"Take a seat. Oh, I'm expecting Father Ted to drop in any time," said Sean. "He's an Irishman," he added, "spent most of the last thirty years living in America."

"America!" replied Trev. "Republican or Democrat? These days Americans are so polarised in their politics."

"I haven't known him that long and have never bothered to ask him, Trev." Sean went off to the kitchen to make a pot of tea while Colleen and Trev spread out over the sofa making themselves at home. Trev grabbed the newspaper lying on the couch.

"Ha, fake news even here. Dunny paper," he commented, tossing it back to where he'd found it.

"Takes a bit of getting used to your cold winter," shouted Colleen, shrugging her shoulders. "Back in Western Australia it is so much warmer."

"And you won't find any Eskimos there," added Trev. "We can fry an egg on our drive."

"Still a lot warmer here than Ireland," replied Sean, turning up the heat pump. "Brrr, those nights I spent in a police cell I thought I'd freeze to death. Such cold nights and that putrid stink of urine still haunts me even to this day."

"Plenty of public dunnies in Perth to remind you of that smell," laughed Trev.

"But you'd melt in our summers," said Colleen.

"Top of the morning to you," said a cheerful Father Ted as he strolled into the lounge.

"And the rest of the day to you," replied Colleen. "You must be Father Ted."

"That I am," he replied. "So who might you be, if I may ask?"

"My sister Colleen and her husband Trev," yelled Sean from the kitchen. "Good timing, just in time for a cuppa, Father."

"Where the hell did you come from?" probed Trev, who expected people to first knock before they entered a house.

"Came through that door over there," replied Father Ted.

"We're family from across the ditch," explained Colleen.

"The ditch?" Father Ted looked perplexed. "What ditch?"

"Over here in this part of the world they call the Tasman Sea the ditch," replied Colleen. "We'd been in Sydney visiting our son and while we were there thought we might just pop across. Christchurch is only a couple of hours away."

"Well, nice to meet you," replied the Father, extending his right hand.

"Thank Goodness, somebody who doesn't hug and has a firm handshake," barked Trev as he shook the Father's hand firmly, leaving the Father wondering if that had been such a good idea.

"And I wanted to see my brother at least once before I carked it," continued Colleen. "I know it all sounds extravagant but when you live thousands of miles away in Perth, crossing the ditch from Sydney is just like going out for a coffee."

"I understand completely," replied Father Ted. "I lived in the USA where the west and east coasts are thousands of miles apart with different time zones. To get to anywhere you travel long distances. Cities are huge and spread out. I'm pleased you're here especially for Sean's sake. Family is important and the past and paranoia shouldn't keep you apart. There's simply no purpose in life being a recluse. Life is here to enjoy no matter what dangers may lie ahead."

"Good on ya mate, never thought I'd hear a priest say that," quipped Trev. "But don't get too excited, it takes more than that to convert me. I can tell ya. I'm as atheist as they come."

"I couldn't agree more, Father," said Colleen, scowling at Trev, "and I've told Sean this many times but he's worried sick about that red-headed moron who we think murdered Da."

"Knuckles," replied Sean from the kitchen. "He was after me too. I never told you before but he saw me in Sydney. Ha, I managed to lose him and his delinquent friends."

"He chased you?" Colleen looked shocked. "How terrifying. I remember Ma telling me Da was in bits after being chased."

"Course the bugger chased him," roared Trev. "From what I gathered that man was a few stubbies short of a six-pack. After the bombing I daresay there would've be many dipsticks wanting to murder you and your dad, Sean."

"Father, Colleen was telling me that they had a black van across the road from their house and Trev thinks that someone may have been carrying out surveillance," said Sean as he brought in the tea.

"And nothing to do with the Irish," laughed Trev. "That chapter's closed for sure. My guess is the CIA or Aussie intelligence."

"And why would that be, may I ask?" enquired the Father.

"Well you might call Cole and I activists of sorts," smirked Trev. "We've flexed our muscles on a number of occasions. Call us protestors against the USA using Pine Gap and Nurrangar for military operations."

"Pine Gap?" The Father looked interested.

"Been used to spy on foreign countries in every American military operation since the September eleven attacks." Trev shook his head to show his discontentment. "A case of America involving Australia in their dirty little operations."

"It was more than that," added Colleen. "You were lucky the police screwed things up and you didn't go to prison. We're now for sure on their watch list."

"What did you do?" asked the priest.

"Never you mind!" replied Trev.

"You've something against America?" asked the Father.

"I'm against any country that sets up its military installations on our Aussie soil," replied Trev.

"Trev joined the protest movement after the sacking of the Whitlam government in 1975," said Colleen.

"Oh!" Father Ted looked surprised.

"The CIA brought our government down," explained Trev. "How dare they interfere in Australian politics and as an ally?"

"My memory of that event was that it was an internal matter involving your government and a difficult senate," replied Father Ted.

"Na, much more than that," replied Trev. "The USA bases were up for renewal. That wasn't going to happen under the newly elected socialist Whitlam government. Even worse, the deputy PM was considered radical and a leader of the Vietnam moratorium movement. USA decided to step in to protect their interests."

"That's when you became anti-American?" suggested Father Ted.

"I'm against any country wanting to use our land for military purposes," replied Trev. "Sean shares the same view, especially after the problems in Ireland."

"It's not just America, Father. We also were involved in protesting against the leasing of Darwin Port to China," added Colleen. "The Chinese are now our biggest worry these days."

"I'd agree with that," replied Father Ted. "Just remember if it hadn't been for America, Australia and New Zealand would be part of the Japanese empire. You need an American presence in the Pacific and China Sea with China looking to expand its influence."

"What on earth were they thinking?" continued Trev. "It was dumb to lease a port so strategic to Australia's defence and it's the terminal for all our undersea data cables."

"Oh dear," commented Father Ted. "Doesn't at all seem the smartest of moves."

 "Oh Sean," said Colleen in a more serious voice. "Just before Da was murdered he phoned us from a phone box. We had a long chat..."

"Yeah, that's right," interrupted Trev. "From what he said, the CIA may have helped the Shankill Butchers. They'd have had the resources to trace your family to Sydney."

"What, the CIA?" Sean looked startled. "Are you sure? How can that be?"

"Da had been thinking about the letter he'd sent to the solicitor and on reflection he just couldn't see how Knuckles would've found out," continued Colleen. "It had to be something else."

"Neither could Ma and I. At the time it seemed ludicrous," Sean commented. "We thought Da was fluthered."

"He did like his Guinness," agreed Colleen. "Anyhow Da told me on the phone that the CIA had been running a clandestine operation, supplying weapons to the IRA and he was aware of several operatives within their cell groups," continued Colleen. "Just imagine if the British had found out at the time?"

"The CIA? I doubt it," replied Father Ted, shaking his head. "As I recall, the IRA were receiving weapons from Gaddafi in Libya and also from a Colombian Marxist drug running cartel. But the CIA? Now that's absurd. They were certainly not on the side of Colombian drug runners nor Gaddafi."

"Are you sure about that?" asked Trev. "A number of IRA weapons smugglers in the 1980s claimed they'd been supplied by the CIA."

Father Ted shook his head. "Look, at the time the British would have dearly loved to have proven CIA involvement and stopped the flow of financial support from the Irish diaspora in the USA."

"Exactly," replied Trev. "So we agree at least then that the British wanted to discredit the CIA who they believed were gun smuggling?"

"It now makes a lot of sense," added Sean. "When we were never held accountable for the bombing some people, maybe the CIA, might have thought we'd become informants."

"Precisely what Da was thinking," added Colleen. "You both knew too much and had to be silenced. He thought the CIA may have assisted the Shankill Butchers in finding us. They often get others to do their dirty work."

"So what's your story, Colleen?" asked Father Ted, conveniently changing the subject.

"What do you mean, my story, Father?" Colleen asked. "I had nothing to do with the IRA, thank goodness, but because of Sean and Da I have been made to suffer."

"Sorry, I mean your story about what happened after the bombing. Sean and your cousin Paddy told me their stories."

"Is Paddy here?" asked Colleen.

"I met with him last week," Sean replied. "I guess I can arrange a meeting for you."

"Please do," replied Colleen. "I'd like to see that little rascal again. So you'd like to hear my story, Father?"

"I would indeed," replied Father Ted, making himself comfortable in the armchair.

"I recall a cold January afternoon when Da and Sean left the house. We knew they were up to something. Mum and I used to do a bit of earwigging outside the door to the back room where Da and Sean would spend some time. Quite effective when you put a glass to the door and put your ear on it. We suspected they were making a bomb because it wasn't the first time they had done this sort of thing."

"A bomb?" Father Ted looked across at Sean, frowning.

"Over the last few days," continued Colleen, "both had been very quiet, too quiet, and Da had been particularly affectionate towards Ma. That's how we knew something major was up. When they didn't come home that night Ma became very distressed expecting the worst. She was in bits—a mess, so we went around to see her brother who had a sympathetic ear. They were very close, you know. It was the next day that the Garda visited and suggested we move house for our own safety. They told us that Da and Sean were alive but locked up. Later we learned that as a family we had to simply disappear and tell no one. Can you believe that? To just walk away from friends and family without a word."

"It had to happen for our own safety," interjected Sean.

"Your safety," Colleen continued. "As a teenage girl they expected me to just walk away and leave my friends. I can tell you that I wasn't going without a fight but that's what happened anyway. I finished my education in Australia and it was during that time I met Trev."

"As handsome as ever," interjected Trev. "She was lucky."

"I'm Irish," replied Colleen laughing. "We got married and moved to Perth where Trev had secured a good job."

"Married in a Catholic church, I hope?" said Father Ted.

"Trev's an atheist, Father. They allowed us to have a private ceremony there and that's all. Da wanted to keep everything hush, hush."

"You never thought about God and the intelligent design of man, Trev?" asked the Father.

"Don't go there," replied Trev. "I have no time for bible bashers."

"Trev, be respectful," chastised Colleen.

"I never knew what the rest of the family went through. We had to be careful as any communication could be tracked." Colleen pulled out a handkerchief. "I never knew about Da until much later and Sean didn't tell me about Ma until just before he left for Christchurch."

"They were troubling times and there were reasons for that," replied Sean.

"I know," replied Colleen, "but we seemed safe in Perth."

"The black van," reminded Trev.

"That had nothing to do with Ireland," replied Colleen.

"Yeah, I'm sure it's CIA related," said Trev. "They won't even give us visas to visit the USA."

"I will be visiting there myself next week," said Sean.

"Sorry?" replied Colleen.

"You'd be lucky!" Trev smirked.

"Good for you. About time you left this bubble," said Father Ted.

"After the success of my last book there's a USA publishing company wanting to publish my next book," added Sean. "They want to meet me over there to sort out the book and contract. All expenses paid for."

"You're dreaming, mate," said Trev. "You think they'll let somebody like you into the USA especially after the Waihopai Spy base incident and then there's the more recent events. No way, you've got to be dreaming."

"What incident?" asked Father Ted. "You told me that you were just a protester, Sean."

"He did what?" Trev looked surprised. "He's in it just as thick as I am but I'm sure that the intelligence services are more interested in discovering our sources in the US."

"Sources?" Father Ted glared at Sean again.

Chapter Thirteen

"If you doubt yourself, then indeed you stand on shaky ground."

Henrik Ibsen

"**W**hat's happening?" demanded Trev, as Sean walked into the kitchen the next morning to grab some breakfast. Colleen and Trev were seated at the kitchen table finishing off some cereals, having raided the pantry.

"Happening where?" asked Sean as he put two bagels into the microwave to warm up.

"Well, you've got the wheels haven't you?" suggested Trev as he raised his cup to sip more of his coffee.

"Give the man a break, Trev. At least let him sit down first and have his breakfast. Do you want a cuppa, Sean?" asked Colleen. "The jug's just boiled."

"I'll get myself a cuppa tea, thanks," replied Sean. "We could go into town this morning." Sean carefully removed his warm bagels out of the microwave and found a seat at the table. "But we do have Father Ted coming around this afternoon…"

"Hell, not him again and more bible bashing," complained Trev. "Hasn't the man got a life?"

"He's bringing Paddy. You did say you wanted to see him, Colleen." Sean sunk his teeth into a bagel.

"Sounds good to me and I assure you Trev will be on his best behaviour won't you?" Colleen scowled in Trev's direction. "I'm really looking forward to meeting Paddy, that little rascal. It's been such a long time." Colleen sighed.

"Ha, the city that rocks," suggested Trev.

"Sorry?" replied Sean.

"Christchurch, the city that rocks," repeated Trev.

I wouldn't know about that, though I'm sure we have our share of night clubs," laughed Sean. "Did you want to go clubbing tonight?"

"Na, too old for that stuff, though a beer or two would go down well if you're shouting. I meant all the earthquakes Christchurch has," clarified Trev. "It's a wonder that the South Island hasn't just sunk back under the Pacific Ocean."

"Well, we've got you pushy Aussies to thank for that and we're mighty grateful," laughed Sean. "The Australian tectonic plate is actually causing the South Island to rise, not sink. As for the earthquakes, they've been and gone in Christchurch. It's been at least nine or ten years now."

"Still the Shaky Islands," joked Trev. "That's what we call it in Aussie. You're on the ring of fire and have already lost most of your continent to the sea."

"We've been called many things but most people here seem to be happy with just being called New Zealand, despite the media and government trying to tell us otherwise." Sean sipped his tea.

"Bloody indoctrination it's everywhere," sighed Trev. "Whatever happened to quality journalism and reporting? Some say television was invented to indoctrinate and control the masses."

"It's social media," said Colleen. "Mainstream media these days can't compete."

"So they churn out a lot of crap," Trev snorted. "Eventually most people will surf the web and programme their own daily viewing."

"And where does that put the fake news channels then?" Sean asked

"Down the dunny, Sean, where they belong," laughed Trev. "I'd love to be the one to push the flusher."

"And you would if you could," laughed Colleen. "You can see, Sean, it's a full time job for me just managing this scallywag. He's quite a handful with something to say on every topic."

"Well, he'll soon be able to stretch his legs out in town," laughed Sean. "But not much to see now that most of the earthquake damaged buildings have been repaired or demolished. Still a few packing crates around though, to support some buildings, as well as a lot of empty sections."

"It caused quite a bit of damage then?" Colleen asked.

"Did it ever? The cathedral in particular is still in disrepair."

"Little point fixing that," commented Trev. "Who goes to church these days anyhow?"

"You still go to mass don't you, Sean?" enquired Colleen.

"I do, and Father never lets me miss a week. He thinks I need to confess my sins and seek forgiveness."

"He's got a hard job there," laughed Trev.

"That's where Paddy recognised me," replied Sean. "As for the cathedral, since the earthquake it's been a hot topic. A number of Anglicans wanted to demolish and replace it with a modern cathedral, although most Cantabrians favoured restoration since the church is of the Gothic era. They may not go to church but they love their cathedral." Sean rose from the table. "Anyhow, will everyone be ready in fifteen minutes to go for a ride to town?"

"I'm ready to go now," replied Trev.

Colleen and Trev left to fetch some jackets as they were not used to cold winters. They returned five minutes later.

"Let's be off then," said Sean as he drove out of the garage with his two passengers.

Susie watched from her garden as the car backed down the drive.

"I bet Susie would love to know where we're off to," Sean chuckled.

"A nosey neighbour?" asked Trev.

"Is she ever? And she didn't like what I had to say about China in my last novel. She was even more upset when I told her my next novel is all about how the CCP are destroying China," Sean laughed.

"And they are," commented Trev.

Sean continued driving towards town while Trev and Colleen made the most of looking at the houses as they drove past.

"We get a lot of South Africans in Perth," said Colleen.

"They leave South Africa because it's now apartheid against the white and coloured," clarified Trev.

"Sounds like Northern Ireland don't you think, Colleen?" Sean commented.

"The discrimination was much worse in Northern Ireland. We were treated very badly," replied Colleen. "The best council housing and jobs went to the Protestants."

"Perth provides a comparable climate for the South Africans and in Australia people are treated equally with none of this special treatment bullshit," added Trev.

"This is Colombo Street, the main street in Christchurch," informed Sean as he turned into a busier road.

"I thought so," replied Trev.

"You know Christchurch?" Sean looked surprised.

"No, I thought that car was following us. Take the next turn left, we'll see for sure," instructed Trev.

Sean pulled into the left hand lane waiting for the traffic light to change.

"Good," said Trev. "There's a car between us. Put your foot down quickly on the green light and take the first right."

"Trev knows what he's doing," commented Colleen. "He's done this before in Perth."

"He has?" Sean looked surprised.

The light changed and Sean took off with a screech. He turned right at the next road.

"Good," said Trev. "Now park the car in between those two cars."

"But that's across a driveway," said Sean.

"Just do it," ordered Trev.

Sean concealed his car between the two parked cars and they waited. Shortly afterwards a grey car turned down their street and sped past. They waited until the car was out of sight.

"Now do a U-turn and we should be fine," instructed Trev.

"I'll park in the shopping centre car park," said Sean, "and we can walk from there into town."

"Good idea," replied Colleen. "Have you never been followed before?"

"I'm usually too busy driving to notice," said Sean, "and I wouldn't have known if Trev hadn't told me."

Sean parked in the shopping centre car park and the three of them walked down Colombo Street towards town.

"Town used to be much busier," said Sean, "but after the earthquake a lot of businesses and government departments never returned. Most of the high-rise buildings were damaged and demolished and weren't replaced as many people developed elevatophobia and megalophobia."

"Right mate. Whatever," responded Trev.

"Which is what?" asked Colleen.

"The fear of lifts and the fear of tall buildings. You can imagine how scary it must have been for those working six or more storeys high when the big earthquakes hit and it was probably worse for those in a lift at the time. Then more recently we have had all the lockdowns with Covid, which added to the damage already done to the central city. Many who'd been working in town and elsewhere are now working from home. Inner-city businesses have been struggling."

"And still are in many cities worldwide," commented Colleen. "Many of those now working from home realise they can own much nicer and cheaper accommodation outside the big cities."

"I'll show you the new bus exchange building, one of our new buildings following the earthquake," Sean said as he attempted to cross the road before changing his mind.

"I think that we should cross further up at the pedestrian crossing where it's safer," suggested Colleen.

"This is Christchurch, not Sydney. It's very safe, not much traffic here," Sean said, arrogantly stepping out again onto the road and beginning to cross.

"Look out!" Trev cried, stretching out and dragging Sean back towards the pavement as a speeding car appeared from nowhere, missing Sean by inches.

"Da, Ma then you, next it'll be me," whimpered Colleen.

"So you think they were trying to kill me?" asked a shaken Sean.

"It looked that way," replied Colleen.

"Na, just a young guy trying to be macho. You know, the loud exhausts, and screeching take-off," replied Trev. "We all did it in our day."

"So you saw the driver?" asked Sean.

"Yeah, but he wasn't Irish if that's what you're asking," Trev replied. "Looked more Asian, say early twenties?" "Guess that the car could have been the same one that followed us before."

"Then it might have been deliberate," said Colleen.

"Dunno about that," Trev replied. "Shit happens. There are all sorts of dipsticks on the road these days."

A shaken Sean continued to show them around central Christchurch before returning to the comfort and security of his house. Trev and Colleen chatted to Susie while Sean put the car away into the garage.

"So what's for lunch? We often get the barbie firing back in Perth." said Trev, smacking his lips. Colleen gave him a chilling look.

Sean walked to the fridge and pulled out a plastic container. "These cold days I usually have a bowl of soup and a slice of bread," he said. "Home-made soup and none of that packaged rubbish," he added. "You know it's processed foods that are killing people."

"Nice one," replied Colleen. "Can I do anything to help?"

"No, it's all sorted. It just requires heating." Sean put a pot on the stove and three bowls on the table.

"Susie offered to take a family photo," Trev said after he'd slurped a mouthful of soup off his spoon. "Hm, could do with a bit more salt," he complained.

"She can be a kind oul soul at times," replied Sean. "She likes to give gifts, I think she believes it will bring her good luck."

"Oh yes, don't the Chinese like to gamble," laughed Trev. "Well they do in our casinos."

"So what time is Paddy coming?" asked an excited Colleen.

"Probably in about half an hour," replied Sean.

They finished their meal, after which Colleen offered to stack the dishwasher. Colleen then moved into the lounge where she eagerly watched out the window in anticipation of Paddy's appearance. Trev spread himself out on the couch and turned on his laptop.

"Ha, one of our informants—the staffer, has committed suicide," announced Trev. "Apparently found dead still with his wallet in his pocket."

"Not surprised," replied Sean from the kitchen. "It does seem to happen in the USA. Just like that feller Epstein when the security cameras just happened to be on the blink and his cellmate just happened to be moved out. Another suicide of course."

"So, you're sure you still want to go to the States?" teased Trev. "

"Not really, but with publishing these days you have to grab any opportunity you can," said Sean coming into the lounge. "The problems too many books in circulation. If you want to be known then you need the marketing expertise of a publishing company."

"And most publishing companies will only touch those authors who are celebrities, even if their writing is rubbish," added Trev, "and it often is."

"Exactly, and of course it's also got to be politically correct" added Sean.

"Here they are," announced Colleen, as a car pulled up outside the house. She sprang up from the couch and raced to the door. "Paddy!" she cried with tears of joy. She ran down the path and gave him an all-encompassing hug.

"Glad to know you're alive and well," replied an embarrassed Paddy who'd never before experienced a woman throwing herself onto him in that manner.

"Oh I missed you guys," said Colleen as she wiped her eyes with a handkerchief. "And your brothers and sisters?"

"All six of them are back in Belfast," Paddy said. "Do you plan to visit them?"

"I'd like to," replied Colleen.

"How can you?" snorted Sean. "You go back and you're dead meat."

"Things have changed," replied Paddy. "Sure there might still be some holding old scores…"

"…But they're nothing to do with me," said Colleen. "It's your mess, Sean. A mess that you and Da created. I had to suffer all these years for something I never did."

"It was a battle that had to be fought and you should be grateful that some of us stepped up to be heroes," replied Sean.

"Violence is not the answer," commented Father Ted, shaking his head.

"Well, sometimes you have to take matters into your own hands, especially when bad decisions are made by jerks at the top," said Trev. "Unlike humans, you never see a herd of cows electing the dumbest for their leader."

"That's right," laughed Sean.

"Jesus achieved change through peaceful means," continued Father Ted. "There is no need for violence."

"Don't give me Jesus," growled Trev.

"We missed you," said Paddy, changing the subject. "When your family suddenly disappeared we thought the worst. How long are you here for?"

"Just a couple more days," replied Colleen.

"I thought you said your sister, Siobhan knew," probed Sean.

"Not then. Not till much, much later," replied Paddy.

"How could she have known anyway?" Sean probed.

"I told her but that was much later after both Da and Ma had been killed," replied Colleen.

"You told her! It was you?" Sean looked angrily at her.

"Then you could've told the rest of us as well," said Paddy. "All those years of grieving. If only we'd known you were safe."

"I couldn't. I'd never have forgiven myself if Sean had ended up murdered because of me," said Colleen. "I waited until it was safe then just told Siobhan in confidence. We were close and after all those years I just had to share it with her."

"All those years. We started to believe that Uncle Danny had turned informant," said Paddy. "It was terrible and it was what everyone was thinking at the time. There was a lot of talk about moles in the IRA."

"And CIA involvement," said Colleen. "Da and Sean knew too much and we think the CIA may have passed on their whereabouts to the gang."

"Oh! The CIA were working with the IRA?" Paddy looked surprised.

"And no doubt MI5 had moles planted in the IRA as well. We even found a mole in our protest group, planted by the Australian Secret Service," added Trev. "He got a short shrift I can tell you."

"What protest group was that?" asked Father Ted.

"Never you mind," snapped Trev.

"Well, the CIA is not my problem, surely not after all this time when their involvement is now just history," said Sean.

"You've gotta be kidding mate," snarled Trev. "You're in it just as deep as us. I'm not at all surprised about the black van."

"Somebody is at the door," said Colleen. "Can you get it, Trev? Sean's rather nervous answering the door and I don't blame him."

Trev reluctantly rose and returned with Susie.

"I've come to take family photo," she said, producing a camera.

"Thanks a million," replied an appreciative Colleen.

"Do you think it wise to have your picture taken?" asked Father Ted.

"And you were telling me the other day how important family was," teased Sean.

"OK, go ahead but I don't want to be in the photo," said Father Ted.

Susie took several frames before leaving.

"Family is very important," said the Father, "but Susie now has a photo of all of you and what say she is a Chinese spy?"

"A spy? Her?" Trev looked concerned. "Are you sure?"

"Well," continued Father Ted, "she loves the CCP and works for the Chinese embassy. Then there's the security cameras she had installed on her house and on Sean's."

"Oh!" Colleen looked worried. "In more recent times we've been protesting over Chinese intrusion into the Pacific like the Darwin Port lease. Maybe it wasn't such a good idea."

"And," continued Father Ted, "Sergeant did a check on that van parked across the road and concluded surveillance was more likely to be on Susie."

"Speculation," laughed Sean. "Look, she's just a little harmless, old Chinese lady. She's no spy even if at times she is nosey."

"And not the only one at that," snapped Trev.

"She promised she'd have your photo printed before you leave and you will," said Sean.

"Then Colleen, just remember not to use China as a stopover in your overseas travels just in case she turns out to be a spy," joked Paddy. "That's when you return to Ireland."

"You're still a little rascal," laughed Colleen.

"Father, I was wondering, would you be able to take me to the airport on Saturday next week?" Sean asked.

"So you're still going on the big trip to the USA then? Good for you. Time you left the worries of the past behind and moved on. Of course I can take you," replied Father Ted.

Chapter Fourteen

*"Avoiding danger is no safer in the long run than outright exposure. Life is either a
daring adventure or nothing."*
— Helen Keller

Sean tried to relax as Father Ted drove him to the airport but in the end his
nerves won out. He started to fidget, checking and rechecking his carry-on
luggage to confirm he had his money, passport and the necessary papers.

"Are you a bit stressed?" enquired the priest. "From my own experience
you'll be fine once you're on the plane."

He hadn't known the Father for that long but he had found him to be
supportive, empathic and quick to pick up on body language.

"I'm not at all looking forward to being outside my comfort zone,"
responded Sean. "It brings back so many bad memories."

"Bad memories?" probed the priest.

"Well, Father, it was unsettling not knowing what the Garda had planned for
us when we were smuggled out of the country as if we were criminals. Then
after having to flee from Northern Ireland, it was the same again from
Sydney, then finally from Auckland. Perhaps once again I'm in the process
of escaping, this time from Christchurch. The situation here has gone from
bad to worse with Paddy's sister now wanting to visit."

 "Oh dear, you need to leave the past behind," reassured Father Ted. "I'm
so glad you've taken this step, it's what you need to move out of your
comfort zone. I'm sure the Virgin Mary is watching over you as it looks like
your gamble paid off."

"What gamble?" questioned Sean.

"Well, you've been blessed with a beautiful sunny morning. What was your
back-up plan had the plane been grounded due to fog?" asked Father
Ted. "It does happen quite often in Christchurch and people miss their
connecting flights."

"Oh! I never thought about that," replied Sean. "I guess that everything
came upon me at once and I haven't had a chance to think straight. At least
I seem to have all my paperwork and of course my wallet and passport."

"So from Auckland you fly to the Big Apple? What time does your flight leave?"

"I have plenty of time. It's not until 4pm and would you believe it I arrive at the John F Kennedy International Airport about the same time on the same day," replied Sean. "Now that's quite a conundrum."

"Ah, very Irish," laughed the priest. "Haha, Groundhog Day, the one time you can do two things at the same time." The priest entered the drop-off zone at Harewood Airport. "And you say you're flying all that way for just one week?"

"And a sixteen hour flight at that but a week's more than enough," replied Sean nervously. "America these days is not the safest of countries."

"I agree, New Zealand being safe is quite unique in that respect." Father Ted pulled up at the drop-off area.

Sean apprehensively left the car and removed his bag from the boot.

"Well, good luck and enjoy the experience," said Father Ted. "I'll see you in a week's time. Now just relax and make sure you enjoy yourself."

"That I will indeed," replied Sean nervously as he put his bags onto an airport trolley and waved goodbye to the Father.

Sean wheeled his bags to the check-in then wasted no time passing through security to the domestic departure lounge. He was relieved to be left with just his carry-on luggage to worry over and even more relieved when he was able to board his flight. The thought of arriving in Auckland was troubling though, especially as the plane drew closer to Auckland. He associated Auckland with his mother's murder but surely after all these years he would have fallen off any hit list and there'd be no one waiting to pop him off. He reassured himself that Auckland was a quick stop over and it was simply a case of leaving one plane to board another.

At Auckland he followed the passengers disembarking to the baggage carousel. Once he had been reconnected with his check-in luggage he grabbed some lunch at the Domestic terminal then walked the ten minutes to the International terminal. He remembered the story about the famous American Sheriff, Wild Bill Hickok, as he found a seat with its back to the wall. Wild Bill would always sit with his back to the wall so he was ready for any trouble coming his way. One fateful day Wild Bill Hickok could only find a spare seat facing away from the door and was shot in the back of the head. Sean nervously watched and waited for his flight check-in to open. Finally he was able to check his baggage in and was given his seat number.

"You're lucky," said the young woman at the check-in. "You have a window seat. Most people pay extra so they're usually all taken."

"I'm Irish," laughed Sean. The young lady smirked.

Sean wasted no time passing through security into the departure lounge. Now he felt safe and secure and more relaxed, even if he had over an hour to wait before boarding. The hour passed slowly but gave him the opportunity to observe the other passengers. Seriously though, would anybody follow him to the Big Apple?

After finding his seat on the plane he made himself comfortable for the marathon journey ahead. As Father Ted had said he now felt more relaxed. It didn't seem so bad, he thought as he sat there and had a flashback to his first time on an aeroplane. It was following another of those cold Northern Irish nights shivering in the police cells. He recalled finally managing to drift into a deeper sleep only to be rudely awoken and marched off with his dad. At the time he feared they were being led away to be tortured, something not unheard of at the time in Northern Ireland. This seemed even more of a possibility as they were locked up in the back of a black unmarked van. Sometime later, the van stopped and Sean expected the worst. After being released from the van, they were escorted to a large building. He later found out this was the Aldergrove Airport terminal. To his surprise and relief, there waiting for them stood his mother and sister. With eyes full of tears, he had thrown himself into his mother's open arms. His sister was far from accommodating though, stepping back and resisting any hug. Instead she accused both Danny and Sean of ruining her life and was most reluctant to board the plane with them. During the flight to Australia Sean curled up into a ball on his seat and experienced his best sleep for many days. No longer did he have to tolerate the rampant smell of urine and the freezing nights in a cold concrete cell. The next morning he had to be woken for breakfast. It was the best food he'd had since being incarcerated.

"So you're off for a holiday in the Big Apple?" enquired a smartly dressed middle-aged man in a Scottish accent. He had taken the seat next to him.

"Ha, more like business," replied Sean, snapping out of his trance and surveying his travel companion. He looked pretty innocuous, Sean concluded.

"Oh! So what type of work would that be?" asked the Scot.

"I'm a writer," answered Sean. "Off to see my publisher. So are you on business?"

"You could say that," replied the Scot. "My work takes me all around the world."

"You're not in business class?" Sean enquired.

"Sadly, not today," was the passenger's response.

"So what work would that be?" Sean asked.

"This and that, working for governments. So what sort of stuff do you write then?" the Scottish man enquired.

"Conspiracy theory, spy thrillers, you know, that sort of genre," said Sean.

"Oh indeed. One of my favourite types of books," replied the Scot. "You wouldn't by chance have one of your books on you?"

"Indeed I do," said Sean, reaching into his hand luggage tucked under the seat in front. "In fact this is my latest." Sean handed him the book.

"Good, something to read on this long journey." The Scot produced a pair of spectacles and started reading. Sean picked up the remote for the screen in front of him and began to explore the movies and games in the offering.

Shortly after the plane took off a somewhat apprehensive Sean was on a new adventure. Whether it would make him or break him remained to be seen. However, this opportunity as an author was too good to turn down.

It didn't seem that long after the plane had departed that the aircrew started handing out the evening meal. The Scot put his book down, marking his page with his boarding pass. He checked out the meal on the tray in front of him.

"Not bad," said the Scot as he set up his meal.

"I agree, quite tasty," replied Sean, having tried some of the beef.

"No, I mean your book. At places it's quite gripping and hard to put down, especially at this stage when I'm now well into it. What amazes me though is that you seem to know an awful lot about covert American operations, things I would've thought were top secret."

"You would?" Sean looked surprised. "Maybe I'm a spy," he joked.

The Scot frowned. "Yes, things like the USA now having Russia's most advanced anti-aircraft missile, the Pantsir S-One."

"The Americans acquired that from Libyan forces," replied Sean, who was eying up another piece of beef on his tray.

"And the CIA involvement in psycho-electric weapons and remote mind control. How do you know this to be true?" The Scot looked curious.

"That's common knowledge. They were involved in these types of experiments many years ago and it's hardly likely that they've ever stopped despite the negative reaction by the American public. Look, I'm just a fiction writer." Sean loaded his fork with some tasty food. "What I don't know, I make up."

"Hearing aids designed to give fatal strokes?" probed the Scot. "Really?"

"Made up, as I said I'm a fiction writer," laughed Sean. "But it's highly likely. Hearing aids amplify radio waves so you only need to get the right pitch and volume, I would've thought."

"Some writers get their information by researching in libraries. So where do you source all yours from?" The Scot buttered his bun.

"All over the place," laughed Sean. "Even passengers on aeroplanes may make good characters."

"How about social media; places like Wiki-leak or other sources leaking information?" asked the Scot.

"Wiki-leak! Now that's a shame," replied Sean. "That Julian Assange shouldn't be locked away in an English prison when he's just a journalist reporting leaked information like any other journalist. The only difference is that he's spreading truth, not lies."

"So it's OK to publish leaked classified information then?" asked the Scot.

"Journalists, television channels, they all do it and most times the politicians don't seem to mind as they do a lot of leaking themselves," Sean laughed. "But Assange, a political prisoner, doesn't say much for English democracy and the USA demanding his extradition is just as bad. I've experienced what was called English democracy in Northern Ireland so this comes as no surprise."

"The battle of Bannockburn had to be our finest day," bragged the Scot. "In Scotland we stood up to the English and put them in their place and we had smaller numbers in the field."

"But not in the battle of Flodden, that was a real stuff up," smirked Sean. "I believe that in that battle you had the numbers but were outsmarted by the English."

"OK, so there are wins and losses but at least we stood up to the English. So anyway, where do you source all your information from?"

"These days there are lots of Wiki-leak type sources and many more just like Edward Snowdon. America's like a rusty old tin can with leaks coming out everywhere. There are even American politicians eager to leak lies about their opponents to the American Press who, unlike Assange, will never be held accountable." Sean put a mouthful of beef mixed with vegetables into his mouth.

"Have you been to America before?" asked the Scot.

"This is my first time," replied Sean.

"Really? So you don't know anyone in the Big Apple, then?"

"No, I'm just meeting up with my publisher," replied Sean. "Why?"

"Well, be warned," continued the Scot. "Have all your paperwork in your hand. The authorities are very gun conscious and a hand reaching into a pocket could be perceived as reaching for a gun."

"Thanks for the advice," responded Sean. "From what I've heard they shoot first and ask questions later."

"You're onto it lad," replied the Scot, laughing. "I don't mind if you tag along with me to get your luggage. It's a big airport and so easy to get lost."

"Thanks," replied Sean. "I'll take you up on that offer."

The hostess came and cleared away the meal trays and the Scot returned to his book. Sean put a movie onto his entertainment screen and settled back in his seat to watch it. He found it somewhat difficult given the small screen and the discomfort of having to wear ear plugs. Several hours later the lights in the plane were dimmed and the passengers were asked to pull down their blinds, though it was still daylight outside. I guess, thought Sean, when you're travelling one day into another it's the airlines prerogative to play God and choose night and day.

Sean reclined his seat and tried to position himself into a comfortable position to sleep but as he found out there was no comfortable position. It now seemed absurd, on reflection, that on the flight from Belfast he had managed to sleep like a baby. Similarly, the Scot was just managing to doze with some difficulty. Some passengers had the luxury of an empty seat next to them and had more room to spread out and be comfortable. As the plane continued its long journey across the Pacific, both Sean and the Scot sank into a deeper sleep and only started to awaken as the cabin crew began to restore the lighting on the plane. Breakfast was served shortly afterwards.

"Thank you, I've completed your novel," said the Scot, smiling and handing Sean the book back, "and I thoroughly enjoyed it."

"That's a comfort," chuckled Sean. "It's always nice to know if people will still be speaking to me after reading one of my books."

"Though, I have to say it again. It is mind-boggling where you get all your information from. You must do an awful lot of research and I'd have thought some of it was classified and not intended for public release. Now, are you sure that you don't have a direct line to the Pentagon by any chance?" he joked.

"No such luck," replied Sean. "Wouldn't that be nice? As I've said, I'm a fiction writer and the information is made up or out there in the public domain."

"So when's your next novel out?"

"Imminently," replied Sean. "It's the reason for my trip."

"What's it about?"

"Ha," laughed Sean. "You'll have to wait until it's published to find out."

"How long are you in the Big Apple for?" asked the Scot

"One week" Sean said, as he reached into his hand luggage to grab a pen.

"Just one week to see the Big Apple?" The Scot looked surprised. "Customs will be viewing you with suspicion then."

"Why?" asked Sean.

"Well, the American authorities can be so black and white in how they see things. To them a long trip for just one week might suggest you're carrying drugs, or up to no good."

"Never thought of that," said Sean.

"Then again, who would smuggle goods through customs when the government has left the southern border wide open to drugs and human traffickers?"

"Good point," replied Sean. "They might as well not exist."

"Where are you staying?" continued the Scot.

"Now that I don't know. The publisher has me booked in at some hotel," replied Sean. "I'm being met at the airport."

"Hotels can vary so much in price in the Big Apple. It's a very expensive place to live. Customs will certainly be curious if you have no accommodation but you do have a return ticket?" enquired the Scot.

"Indeed I do," replied Sean.

"Well that's not so bad then," the Scot laughed. "As long as you keep those documents in your hands."

"They're very trigger happy," Sean joked nervously, taking his pen and starting to complete the USA arrival document with all the requested details.

Chapter Fifteen

"There's nothing so bad that it couldn't be worse."

Irish proverb

As the plane started to descend for its landing Sean peered out the window. Below, he could see the tall skyscrapers forming the Manhattan skyline. They seemed to stretch for miles. His ears had started to feel very full and itchy as the plane descended. He started to suck harder on the candy that the air hostess had handed him. He didn't feel great at all, somewhat nauseous and a little inebriated due to his travel companion's generosity. The Scottish man didn't look at all worse for wear, even though he had acquired alcohol from the aircrew at every opportunity and Sean, true to form, was never one to turn down free booze. Perhaps he was paranoid but was the Scottish man really trying to get him drunk? Maybe he just wanted to prove Scots could handle their liquor better than the Irish. Now in this state, where he was no longer thinking clearly, he had no alternative but to tag along with the Scot. At least he was confident in navigating such a huge airport.

It seemed that no sooner had the plane touched the tarmac that most of the passengers were ready and eager to disembark. Sixteen hours cooped up in a plane is a very long time and stretching their legs, Sean thought, would have been high on their agenda. The plane aisle quickly filled, becoming crowded as passengers squeezed and pressed together. Some were reaching for carry-on luggage from overhead lockers while others waited impatiently for the doors to open. Sean though, was just content to stay in his seat and sober up.

"Crazy, it's the same every time" observed the Scot. "Little point in rushing, they'll still have five or ten minutes to wait for their bags."

Sean nodded as he enjoyed remaining seated as long as possible. He clipped open his seat belt, pleased that the long flight had ended but now apprehensive as he was about to enter an unfamiliar environment. He was in no hurry, though it did seem to be part of human nature for others to jockey for first position regardless. It reminded him of driving on the roads in New Zealand where some people just drove like maniacs, passing everyone. What were they trying to prove? That their car was faster? That they were a great driver? The only thing that they were really proving was that they were an idiot. Ironically they were often caught up at traffic lights and traffic jams or they got busted for speeding.

When the aisles had finally cleared, the Scot and Sean rose from their seats. Leisurely they collected their carry-on luggage from the overhead lockers before making their way towards the plane's exit. In the airport, Sean was pleased to have the Scot beside him to guide him through a massive building and the various protocols on arrival to eventually arrive at the carousel. This was a very large airport terminal and one would never live down the embarrassment should one be waiting for baggage to appear at the wrong carousel.

"There are more than 70 airlines operating out of John F Kennedy," commented the Scot.

"Wow! That's an awful lot," replied Sean. "That's massive but I can believe it. This place is so huge."

"And this is just one of many terminals," added the Scot.

"What?" Sean looked flabbergasted. "There are more?"

They made their way to the carousel, Sean still slightly groggy from both jet-lag and having indulged in consuming too much alcohol. Despite this, he still managed to walk straight. They joined the other passengers, including those who had been first to leave the aeroplane.

"What people don't realise," continued the Scot, laughing. "The bags don't just come straight off the plane onto the carousel. They'll be screening the bags first and identifying any that the customs officers should examine. They already know who's on the plane and if they are a known drug smuggler, terrorist and so forth."

"Ah, so that's why customs have such a good success rate," commented Sean.

"Exactly," replied the Scot. "Half their work is already done for them. And here's another piece of irony," continued the Scot.

"What's that?" asked Sean.

"Usually the bags that go onto the plane last are the bags that come off first. So the personality B people who arrive late to check-in and who miss out on a seat in the departure lounge are not only the first to make the queue onto the plane but are also the first to receive their baggage off the carousel. So even with all the pushing and shoving to get in first, the A types still can't win."

"Haha," Sean laughed.

"Ah, now that's more promising," said the Scot as the first bags appeared on the carousel. First there were only a few bags, then they started to appear thick and fast. Passengers once again selfishly jockeyed for position; this time to be one of the first to retrieve their luggage.

"They never learn," laughed the Scottish man, who suddenly disappeared as he had spotted his bag on the other side of the carousel. Shortly after, Sean spotted his bag and squeezed through other impatient passengers. He grabbed it before it could take another lap. He squeezed back through those still earnestly waiting, carrying his check-in luggage and loading it onto a trolley.

"Mr Sean O'Brien?"

Sean gingerly turned around to face two tall men in dark suits of about forty years of age. One stood on either side of him.

"I am," replied a curious Sean. "And who might you be?"

"Special Agent John Dizon, and this is Special Agent Henry Ford. Do you have any ID?"

"Sure thing." Sean waved his passport that was already in his hand and Agent Dizon handed it to Agent Ford.

 "Have it checked out, Henry."

"Oh, I'll need that," protested Sean. "I've been told to never let my passport out of my sight."

"No worries," replied Special Agent Dizon. "Bring your baggage and come with us." They were followed by an armed policeman. The other passengers barely noticed what was happening as they continued watching for their baggage.

Sean looked around. He hadn't noticed before but the airport terminal was swarming with armed policemen. He felt somewhat paranoid since they all seemed to be looking in his direction as he was led away to an interview room.

"Place all your baggage on this table," instructed the special agent.

Sean nervously complied with the request and watched on as a customs officer opened his case. He now wished he had put a padlock on his check-in luggage as he recalled stories of airport workers attempting to smuggle contraband through baggage under their control.

The female customs officer meticulously removed the contents of his check-in luggage, then his carry-on luggage. It was neatly spread out over the table. Then she checked through each item.

"All good," said the customs officer, turning to Special Agent Dizon with a smile. He was, after all, a very handsome man.

"Empty your pockets slowly," instructed Dizon. Sean noticed an armed policeman, nursing a revolver, at the door and another one on the other side of the room with a revolver in his hand.

"I'm here for the first time in America," said Sean as he nervously removed his wallet, comb, door keys and other contents from his pockets. "I don't do drugs. What seems to be the problem?"

"Right, now stand up straight and spread your legs while we frisk search you," instructed a stern Dizon.

"You've got to be joking," protested Sean as he reluctantly complied.

"He's clean," said the customs officer.

"They tell me the passport is genuine," announced Special Agent Ford as he entered the room. "I had them run several checks just to make sure."

"Hm." Agent Dizon didn't look convinced. He opened the passport and browsed through it. "This says you're a New Zealander but you have an Irish accent."

"I was born in Northern Ireland but have lived in New Zealand for thirty years."

"Hm, X-ray his empty case and his shoes," Dizon instructed the customs officer.

Sean removed his shoes and passed them to her.

"Where's your mobile?" demanded Dizon. "I need your mobile."

"I don't have one," replied Sean. "Never needed one and never wanted one."

"You don't have a mobile?" Dizon looked at Ford disbelievingly since these days everyone had a mobile. "How do you contact other people then?"

"I don't. Why would I want to be a servant to a phone? I'm only here for a week," Sean added.

"A week?" commented Ford, "You flew all this way just for a week. What could you expect to see in the Big Apple in a week? OK, where's your itinerary then and where will you be staying?"

"I don't have an itinerary and I have no idea what hotel has been booked on my behalf," replied Sean.

"You come to New York for just a week, don't have any plans, nor anywhere to stay?" Ford looked dumbfounded.

"Why?" asked Dizon.

"My publisher has organised that."

"What do you plan on doing in New York then?" continued Ford.

"I've come to see my publisher. I'm a writer, look." Sean extended his left hand and reached down to retrieve something on the table from what had been in his bag. The policeman standing by the door suddenly drew his revolver.

"Stop!" ordered Dizon. "Remove your hand slowly, Sir."

"I just wanted to show you this manuscript," said Sean as he produced it. "As I said, I'm here to meet with my publisher. I'm no drug pusher."

Agent Dizon snatched the manuscript from Sean. He flicked through the pages disbelievingly before placing it back on the table.

"How much money are you carrying?" asked Ford.

"About five hundred US, plus I have a credit card," replied Sean. "I figured that with my accommodation paid for that would be more than enough to see me through the week."

The customs officer returned with the empty suitcase and shoes. "All good, Sir," she said. Agent Dizon shook his head as he was still not convinced. He looked towards his colleague to see if he could think of any more avenues for enquiry. Ford returned a blank look.

"Do you have any questions?" Dizon asked the customs officer.

"No, you've asked everything I would have asked," she replied.

Sean nervously bent down and put on his shoes.

The door suddenly opened and a customs officer entered. "Sir, there is a guy out here wanting to see you. He said that it's very important."

Special Agent Dizon grabbed the opportunity and strolled across the room to the door. Sean could just make out the figure of his plane companion, the Scot, standing outside. The two chatted for a few minutes before Dizon returned.

"Right, that's it! He's clean," said Dizon, still somewhat dubious. "Enjoy the Big Apple."

"He can go?" Special Agent Ford asked, looking astonished. "You're letting him go? Are you sure?"

"Yes, it's not who we're looking for," explained Dizon. "He can go."

The customs officer tidily repacked Sean's bags and promptly escorted him out to the exit.

"Thank you," Sean said to the Scottish man standing by the exit. "I don't know how you ever managed that but I'm very grateful."

"It's who you know in this world, my lad," laughed the Scot. "When you're staying just a week and you have no idea where you're staying, it's certainly going to arouse suspicions."

"Is this normal or do I just look furtive?" asked Sean.

"Do you really want me to answer that? You just drew the short straw my lad, it's that simple," chuckled the Scot as they entered the public area of the terminal. "Put it down to the luck of the Irish," he laughed again. "Most unfortunate you weren't born Scottish."

"Sean O'Brien?" enquired an Irish sounding voice.

"I think it must be your transport," said the Scot. "Enjoy the week."

Sean nervously turned around to face a smartly dressed man of about fifty years of age.

Chapter Sixteen

"The heart of an Irishman is nothing but his imagination."
George Bernard Shaw

"Sean, my name is Conor. Did you have a good trip?"

"A gruelling marathon but I made it," replied Sean followed by a yawn.

"You've done well. My job's to show you around the Big Apple until the boss is ready," continued Conor. "He'll meet with you later in the week. The car is outside if you'd like to follow me."

"Sixteen hours is a long time," replied a tired Sean as he struggled to keep up.

Sean followed Conor out of the airport, still stunned at its size and very grateful that he didn't have to navigate his own way out to the exit. They walked for some time to the huge car park. At the steering wheel of Conor's car, patiently waiting, sat a very dark black man of African descent.

"Ah, this is Mohammed who you will see more of," Conor said. "He's from Nigeria."

Sean greeted Mohammed and both he and Conor sat in the back seat after placing his baggage into the boot. At first Sean found the journey scary as the car sped along the opposite side of the road to what he was used to. The lane changing was also very scary but it seemed that American drivers were well practiced. America seemed so different with its tall skyscrapers everywhere, and wide lane roads.

"We have you booked into an older hotel which is quite central. But it is very nice," said Conor, "and being central it will be easier for you to get around. You need to appreciate that accommodation in the Big Apple is extremely expensive. Some apartments are worth millions of dollars. Since covid, working from home has increased and many people have moved to small nearby towns where real estate is just so much cheaper. They can get a much bigger house and in a much friendlier and safer environment to raise a family."

"Look, I appreciate having my airfare and accommodation paid for," replied Sean. "I'm not yet an author selling millions of copies so I wouldn't expect first class accommodation."

"Exactly," replied Conor, "and that's why we've tried to make you as comfortable as we can in an older hotel but one that is central and closer to the attractions."

"Have you been in New York long, Conor?" asked Sean.

"I've been in the New York publishing game for thirty years now and have seen the publishing landscape change significantly in that time. These days, traditional publishers will usually only offer contracts to people who are well known or already successful writers. Writers showing merit might be offered a cost-sharing contract. In your case, given the success of your last book, you just make the cut for costs included," added Conor.

"Thank you," replied Sean.

"Seriously, the competition today with the sheer volume of books being published each year is inconceivable," Conor added. "There's so much talent out there and many five star books are overlooked simply because the writer is an unknown. It's not easy turning talented writers down and occasionally we live to regret it but we're a business and we need to make a profit. For many writers it's a lottery to win the backing of a traditional publisher and for traditional publishers we now have to compete with those supporting self-publishers."

"Ah, but you still have the edge over self-publishers in your branding, distribution channels and know-how, well at least against the smaller self-publishers," said Sean.

"We do to a large extent and we're more professional in the use of artists for cover design as well as in attention to detail such as formatting, editing, proof-reading and content editing," added Conor. "Self-publishers often skimp on the important things like the cover and back page, formatting and on ensuring their book is error free."

"Indeed," agreed Sean. "An author cannot successfully proofread their own book as I found out years ago. It's hard to spot your own errors."

"Exactly, we're on the same page," laughed Conor, "and many of the great books have been proofread many times as even proof readers are fallible."

"I'm surprised to have another Irishman as my guide in a huge country like the USA," Sean commented. "As an immigrant you'll no doubt understand how overcoming I find this enormity?"

"Nothing at all that surprising," laughed Conor. "There are over 40 million Irish in the USA."

"That's more than seven times the population of Ireland," said Sean.

"And in the Big Apple there are over a million here," added Conor. "Many of our American ancestors were called Scotch-Irish because they came here given the promise of greater freedom of religion and land ownership. They were like the South Americans today, economic migrants, looking for jobs and a better life. More importantly I can find you many Irish pubs here where you can find a decent Guinness," laughed Conor. "I'm not sure they'd have supplied that on the plane."

"Now that would be nice," replied Sean. "I'm not impartial to a pint or two of gat between toilet breaks. So you're from Northern Ireland?"

"That I am and Catholic as they come," Conor whispered. "I don't discuss religion in Mohammed's presence."

"I'll keep that in mind. Did you experience the troubles?" enquired Sean.

"That we did," replied Conor. "Like so many others, we left Belfast to get away from it. The USA was our sanctuary and a place where we were treated fairly. Americans have been very sympathetic to the Irish situation. During the conflict, Americans used to pass around a hat in the pubs to collect money for the IRA and IRA prisoners. The greatest amount of money came through Irish charities like the American Ireland fund though."

"So most Irish Americans and American politicians supported the IRA?" suggested Sean.

"Unfortunately that would be a myth, Sean. Most Irish Americans did not but many felt sympathetic and prepared to give financial support when they heard about Bloody Sunday, and Thatcher allowing hunger strikers to die."

"Don't remind me," said Sean.

"As for politicians," continued Conor, "if there was nothing in it for themselves and America then they'd have no interest."

"Typical politicians," commented Sean. "It's amazing how so many American politicians, on their modest government salaries, turn out to be millionaires. Even in New Zealand, politicians often end up with cushy positions after serving the country. Cushy positions, like in the United Nations. Some even receive knighthoods or are made Dames."

"The Irish situation was not good, Sean, and we were treated so badly. They were indeed difficult times in Belfast and they will haunt me to my grave. But enough about Ireland and its upsetting experiences. I just really don't want to go there. It makes me so angry."

"The traffic and sheer number of people are unbelievable," commented Sean as he looked out the window.

"Oh yes, the Big Apple is a very busy place. I think from memory now there's about 19 million people," replied Conor.

"Wow, I guess when you take the population into perspective then the number of shootings doesn't come across as that bad," said Sean.

"Exactly," replied Conor, "And under the Second Amendment of the Constitution everyone is entitled to have firearms."

"And you?" asked Sean.

"I couldn't even kill a spider," laughed Conor. "If I find a spider inside the house I capture it and put it outside. It has a right to life. Not all Americans have guns and there is a strong lobby pushing for changes to the Second Amendment."

"What people fail to realise is that it is people, not guns, that kill others," said Sean.

"So true, and now that we have 3D printers, control is pointless as people can make their own guns," added Conor.

Mohammed brought the car to a stop outside an older but well-kept building. It looked to have once been an expensive hotel but still carried a certain degree of grandeur.

"We're here," announced Conor, opening his door. Sean bounced out and retrieved his baggage from the boot. The two walked into the hotel to the reception where a young lady, barely out of school, handed Sean a key to his room.

"As you can see it is an older hotel and you will notice that more when you see how slow the lift is. Most modern hotels have digital cards instead of keys," commented Conor.

"That's OK," replied Sean, "It's just a bed for the night. Little point having five-star accommodation if you just want somewhere to rest your head."

"Exactly." Conor led Sean into a lift that took them to the fourth floor.

"This is great," said Sean, having opened the door to his room. By the door was a closet to put his suitcase and clothes. There was even a safe. In front of him was a queen sized bed, table and chairs and a wall mounted 35 inch television. The room looked freshly painted and, although quite small and compact, it was more than adequate. He entered the bathroom. The shower looked clean and the vanity unit was modern, not reflecting the age of the building. Sean was very satisfied.

"It may be old but it's a well-maintained hotel," said Conor. "Do you have a copy of your manuscript for the boss?"

"Sure," replied Sean, reaching into his suitcase. "I'm surprised that he wanted a paper copy when I'd already sent a pdf."

"He's old-school," laughed Conor. "These days more and more things are digital. Many people prefer digital versions to actual books but not my boss," he laughed, taking the manuscript. "So breakfast is included but you will have to pay for your other meals. I'm going to leave you now and will catch up with you for lunch about twelve mid-day. I'm sure you're very tired so this will give you a chance to settle in. If you decide to venture outside, I wouldn't wander far. Some areas can be dangerous, especially now with all the political left-wing stupidity of defunding the police."

Sean saw Conor to the door and watched it close behind him. It locked automatically from the outside. He went into the bathroom and downed a glass of water before kicking off his shoes and collapsing his exhausted body onto the comfortable bed. He still felt very groggy and tired from the sixteen hour journey. Sean spread out and lay there prostrate, thinking about the day and the new adventure that lay ahead. After today there were many unanswered questions. Who really was the Scottish man to instruct an FBI agent? Had he been trying to get him drunk for some reason? Maybe he was just paranoid. Then there was the question of why he'd been subjected to interrogation and an extensive search? He didn't buy into the Scot's explanation. Were the American authorities privy to his IRA history or maybe this was related to his anti-American activities in New Zealand? The FBI was no longer the finest police force in the world, having lost all credibility during the Trump presidency. They seemed to be on just another fishing expedition. Sean yawned, and closed his eyes. It had been a long day and being interrogated had been emotionally exhausting. He was looking forward to tomorrow and seeing the sights but now he just needed to doze for an hour before he organised his evening meal. Very soon he drifted into a deep sleep.

Chapter Seventeen

'We're born alone, we live alone, we die alone. Only through our love and friendship can we create the illusion for a moment that we're not alone.''

Orson Welles

The sun was streaming in through the window when Sean awoke from his intended doze. Now feeling much better, it was time for him to investigate the local area and find a restaurant. He was looking forward to his first evening meal in America and he felt very hungry, though he had eaten well on the plane. Father Ted had been right, he needed to get out of his comfort zone. Sean was quite excited at the prospect of being in another country and experiencing their lifestyle. He rolled over to check the twenty-four hour clock next to his bed. Ridiculous; perhaps it hadn't been plugged in as it was showing ten o'clock. He felt sweaty after the plane journey as he rose and made his way to the bathroom. Now somewhat refreshed after a quick shower and a change of clothes he drew the blinds and peered out through the window. It didn't look at all like early evening given the hive of activity: traffic and pedestrians, but this was America. Having decided that it must be morning, ridiculous as it seemed, he headed downstairs for breakfast. Sean strolled into the breakfast room.

 "I'm sorry, Sir, but we closed at nine thirty," said one of the young ladies clearing the tables.

"Oh!" Sean now felt extremely hungry since he had not eaten for 20 hours.

"There are several places where you can still buy breakfast, Sir. Just turn right out the hotel entrance_and follow the sidewalk," continued the young lady.

Sean left the hotel and found a restaurant selling all day American breakfasts. He was most surprised by the size of the meal laid out before him but he was hungry and had no difficulty finding room for the eggs, bacon, sausages, fried potato, waffles and toast on his plate. Before Sean could order a cup of tea, the waitress returned and filled his cup with a complimentary coffee.

He was very thirsty so reluctantly he took a sip of the coffee. It wasn't that bad after all, though he'd sooner have tea. Looking at the menu it looked like they didn't sell cups of tea. This was America and coffee would just have to do. Sean, now content with a full stomach, returned to his hotel room to unpack his suitcase. After unpacking, he explored the hotel to check out the facilities. Being a cheaper hotel he wasn't surprised that it didn't have a swimming pool nor gym but it did have a pub and, better still, Guinness.

Sean checked his watch. Given his late start, the time had flown and was drawing close to twelve mid-day. He needed to head down to the lobby to meet Conor. Down in the reception area he found a selection of newspapers and filled in the time catching up with the news.

"Howya, alright boyo?"

"Oh it's you, Conor," replied Sean lifting his head. "Top of the morning to you."

"You have a good kip?" enquired Conor.

"Did I ever. Slept like a baby," replied Sean. "I must have been asleep for about seventeen hours."

"Seventeen hours, now you're not codding me?" replied Conor, laughing. "Though yesterday when you arrived you did look like you'd seen better days. Perhaps a little fluthered maybe?"

"Jet-lagged not wasted," lied Sean.

"Jet-lag! Oh, a terrible, terrible thing," commented Conor. "Anyhow let's crack on, get some lunch and explore the Big Apple. Guess you'll be hungry if you missed breakfast."

"Oh, I had breakfast, an American breakfast and so much food on the plate."

"That's right," replied Conor. "The biggest meal here in America is breakfast. Hope you have room for lunch, something light like a sandwich or two, then I'll take you to where the twin towers once stood."

They set off down the busy street outside the hotel and found a diner.

"So where were you when the twin towers were hit?" Sean sunk his teeth into a chicken and corn sandwich.

"I certainly wasn't in the twin towers, that's for sure but I was in New York and the place was chaotic at the time. I wouldn't have wanted to be anywhere near those buildings being full of asbestos," said Conor. "There was dust, probably asbestos, everywhere in the air. The buildings were old and it would have cost them a fortune to remove the asbestos."

"Oh! Are you suggesting it was deliberate?" probed Sean. "I thought that terrorists were flying the two planes that hit the buildings."

"Oh, they were and I agree that does make it less likely," said Conor. "But what I do know, based on expert opinions, is that a plane hitting the building shouldn't have been enough to bring those towers down. A number of observers suggested that the building destructions had all the appearance of a controlled demolition."

"I don't understand." Sean looked perplexed. "I mean if the planes were under the control of the hijackers and the buildings were owned, presumably, by Americans, then the two would have to be in collusion. That doesn't seem very likely."

"I know what you're saying," replied Conor. "It's a mystery to this day but then so is a plane bringing down such a solid structure. Believe me there are all sorts of conspiracy theories going around."

"Father Mychal Judge, a chaplain to the New York City Fire Department, was in the twin towers," said Conor on a more serious note.

"Father Mychal Judge?" Sean looked puzzled. "Was he Irish?"

"Absolutely, he was the son of Irish immigrants. He wasn't in the building at the time the planes hit. After he heard that a plane had struck one of the towers of the World Trade Centre he rushed over, entered the lobby and prayed for the rescuers, injured and dead," said Conor.

"Holy Mother of God, he would have got a medal surely for such bravery," said Sean.

"Maybe he might have if he had made it out," replied Conor. "It's so sad there were close to three thousand people who died that day."

"War casualties, I guess" retorted Sean. "There are always civilians killed in war."

"Sorry?" Conor looked shocked. "What do you mean war casualties? This was terrorism. These were innocent people, not soldiers and there were many good Catholics amongst them. How can you be so callous?"

"Well, it's no different to the Irish situation and the IRA fighting back," replied Sean. "In this case the military action had been carried out by Arab soldiers simply bringing the war to American soil."

"Terrorists and cowards you mean," replied Conor. "They were extremists not soldiers."

"It's all about revenge," replied Sean. "Revenge for the wars and turmoil created by the Americans who wanted to steal their oil in their countries. The American people are no less innocent as they put these war mongers into power at the election box."

"Unfortunately, democracy isn't that simple," replied Conor.

"And the same has happened in Ukraine where the war has been deliberately extended at the price of innocent lives. It's been America who has stood in the way of dialogue allowing western oligarchs to buy up land and resources cheaply."

"How can you be so heartless? Nine eleven was an act of terrorism." Conor looked dismayed.

"And America's destruction of the Nord pipelines was not?" blurted Sean.

"So, I take it that you don't feel any compassion towards those who lost friends and families through this cowardly attack on innocent lives then?" concluded Conor.

"Why should I?" snapped Sean. "It's life, some people did something."

"How about Father Mychal Judge who wasn't at the towers when the first plane hit but he went there to comfort and pray for the lives of others?" asked Conor. "Do you feel any compassion towards him?"

"It is sad to see a holy Joe, a good Catholic, dying to save the lives of others," replied Sean, "but that was his choice. He didn't need to go there."

"And there were others like the firemen who went there out of duty to help and who died in an attempt to save others," added Conor. "Do you have any compassion for them? Perhaps when you see the site and memorial you may feel empathetic."

The waitress returned with two bills. Sean didn't have any change so gave her a twenty dollar note to Conor's amusement. He expected her to return with the change.

"Well, shall we go and look at the site?" asked Conor.

"I just need the waitress to return with my change," replied Sean.

Conor laughed. "She would have taken that as a generous tip."

"Oh, I couldn't ask her for my change?" Sean looked annoyed.

"Not now," laughed Conor. "But you'll remember for next time and you made her very happy. Over here people are expected to tip."

Mohammed was waiting in a car to take them to the twin towers.

"What does Mohammed think about the twin towers?" asked Sean after he had driven away. "I'm sure, like us, he would be anti-English with Nigeria once being a British colony and exploited by the English. Then after the English, the Americans took control over their resources like oil. You know, they even have a military presence there, a drone base."

"Are you suggesting that he might not be sympathetic?" asked Conor.

"Just curious," said Sean as they made their way to the memorial and museum. "America interfering in the politics of other countries has made a lot of enemies."

They spent the rest of the day around the tower site and area. Towards the end of the day Conor suggested that they walk back as Sean looked to be fit and sober enough to walk a few miles. There was much more to see on foot.

"Don't look back but I think we're being followed," Conor looked very concerned. "I noticed the same two men when we were at the twin towers."

Sean surreptitiously glanced back and noticed two well-dressed men further back on the footpath.

"Do we need to be worried?" asked Sean. "They don't look threatening, the mugging type."

"Definitely," replied Conor. "Don't be fooled by appearances or be taken in by a pretty woman. Here people carry guns and it is clear, by your dress, that you're a tourist and a worthy target. We should be very worried. These are hard days in America and people are feeling the economic pinch. The men were probably hanging around tourist sites waiting to pick out their next target."

"What do we do?" asked Sean.

"We have to lose them. It's that simple and you certainly don't want them knowing where you're staying; that's if we make it back alive," replied Conor.

"Really, that bad?" whimpered Sean.

"There are murders every day in the Big Apple. Just be prepared to run when I say so. Meanwhile, we'll head into a busier part of the town. We're less likely to be mugged on a crowded street but then these days it happens. We can dive down an alley or two, jump on a bus, or catch a taxi, whatever it takes to lose them."

The two continued to walk into a more public and crowded area. Sean occasionally looked behind. Conor had been right. The two men had turned down the same streets and were most definitely following.

Conor shouted, "Now!" He dragged Sean with him, darting down a narrow alley then through the back entrance to a departmental store. At the other end Conor sighted a bus about to leave and together they ran to catch it just before it pulled away. Having boarded, they looked behind and saw the two men emerging from the store but too late. The bus left, leaving their pursuers standing outsmarted on the sidewalk, unsure what direction Sean and Conor had taken.

Sean and Conor travelled for at least five stops before leaving the bus and continuing on foot back to the hotel.

"I need a beer after that," declared Conor, still huffing.

"The hotel bar has the black stuff," said Sean smiling as they entered the hotel.

The two sat in the bar to catch their breath, each downing a pint of Guinness.

"That's never happened to me before," said Conor. "How about you?"

"It has," replied Sean. "I was once chased by some of the Shankill Butchers."

"Sorry, you were? Such an evil bunch but they got what they deserved in the end," replied Conor.

"Imprisonment?" suggested Sean.

"And the Shankill Pub bombing," added Conor. "That took out two of the gang and another died shortly after from his injuries. Most of them had scars at least to make them think twice. Though it wasn't that pleasant for any Catholic in Belfast after the bombing when the gang went on a killing and maiming frenzy. You're so lucky to be alive."

"Tell me about it," laughed Sean. "The luck of the Irish."

They both laughed and consumed more Guinness as they shared some of their fondest memories of Ireland.

"One thing is for certain, we're going to need to change those clothes of yours," commented Conor.

"I know I might be sweaty but do I smell that bad?" laughed Sean.

"If it comes to sweaty then that makes two of us," chuckled Conor. "You're a sitting target in those clothes, that's what I'm getting at."

"Sorry, sitting target?" Sean looked puzzled.

"You stand out as a tourist and a wealthy one at that," explained Conor. "I just wouldn't fancy your chances wearing those clothes down some of our streets. Look, I'll bring you some clothes tomorrow so you'll look just like a New Yorker. As I said, New York is a dangerous place and even more so by the stupidity of left-wing politicians defunding the police. Just be careful and don't travel on your own too far from the hotel, at least not in those clothes."

Chapter Eighteen

"As you slide down the bannister of life , may the splinters never point in the wrong direction"

An Irish saying.

That night Sean took Conor's advice and didn't venture far from the hotel for his evening meal. He had heard that Americans loved to dine out and found that just down the road there were plenty of restaurants to choose from. The next morning he was awake in time to enjoy the buffet breakfast in the hotel restaurant. They had a wide selection, enabling him to not only include bagels in his diet but also his traditional cup of tea. Once again, Conor was meeting him at mid-day, this time planning on taking him to Times Square and Central Park. As Sean had plenty of time to kill, he made the most of it by settling down in one of the lobby's comfortable imitation-leather armchairs and reading the New York newspapers on offer.

Today the newspapers seemed more about Ukraine winning the war than anything. He remembered advice someone once gave him that whenever there's a big story in the media, they're trying to distract you. But from what? The Biden economy was in terrible shape with the mid-term elections pending. Perhaps that was the reason, given that New York was a Democrat Party State. Or perhaps it was New York's escalating crime rate and…

"How's the form?" Conor appeared from behind Sean.

"After yesterday my legs have seen better days," laughed Sean, raising his head above the paper.

"No hangover then?" teased Conor.

"Yesterday was just a tasting session," laughed Sean.

Conor looked over Sean's shoulders to see what he was reading. "Oh, it's all bad news, it always is," he commented, "and you can never believe all you read these days. You're a fiction writer, you could get a job as a newspaper journalist."

"The Ukraine situation in reality does not look good," replied Sean. "When Trump was elected I remember many people being scared that he might bring about Armageddon. Instead he ended the war in Afghanistan and brought about the Abraham Accords Peace Agreement in the Middle-East. Though he did upset the Iranians using a drone attack to eliminate their top general. It's really Biden and his crazy crowd that we should be worrying about, risking a third world war against Russia and China."

"Agreed," replied Conor. "To put it bluntly, they're caving into the demands of the industrial military complex. The Afghanistan war has ended so now they need another one to make money. One war ends and another begins. It's always been that way in America but as long as it's not on American soil, who cares? Well, do you want to try on these lovely clothes? We don't want you getting mistaken for a tourist now, do we?" Under his arm Conor clutched a large brown parcel which Sean eyed with curiosity.

Sean and Conor returned to Sean's hotel room and Sean tried on the clothes.

"I don't know," Sean appeared unenthusiastic. "These clothes are definitely not me. I don't feel that comfortable in them." He walked over to the mirror to take another look and frowned.

"Well, it's only for a few days," Conor insisted. "We don't want to be mugged and have already had one close call. A little discomfort is a small price to pay for one's safety."

"I guess you're right but they're going to get a lot of getting used to," Sean reluctantly agreed.

"There are enough clothes there to last you the rest of the week," added Conor. "Well, if you get changed then we'll find a nice diner nearby to grab a sandwich. This time we'll be taking a bus as Mohammed isn't available."

Sean changed and the two walked down to a restaurant further down the street. It was one that Sean had gone to for an evening meal.

"Do you know much about Times Square?" asked Conor.

"Not really," replied Sean as he finished his lunch.

"It has a lot of Irish pubs and Irish restaurants," said Conor.

"That's good…and Guinness?"

"Why, of course, Sean. It wouldn't be an Irish pub without it." Conor laughed and walked over to a bus stop with Sean following. The bus soon arrived and they were on their way. Sean had always wanted to see Times Square and was looking forward to this new adventure.

"We'll get off here," said Conor as the bus drew to a stop. "I want to show you where our world famous FBI are located." They left the bus and stopped across the road to look at the skyscraper housing the FBI.

"That's one big police station," commented Sean as he tried to count the floors but gave up.

"Over two thousand FBI agents in New York," added Conor, "but when you take into account the population of New York then it doesn't sound that many."

"But you do have the NYPD as well?" asked Sean.

"We do indeed and the Central Park Precinct also. They patrol Central Park," added Conor as he started to walk down the road. Sean followed and eventually they arrived at Times Square.

"Now, this is our most famous landmark," said Conor as the neon lights and billboards came into sight. This is where all the tourists go. Flashing lights and crowds seem to draw people, especially tourists."

"Then why did I need to dress like a New Yorker?" asked Sean. "I'll certainly stick out in this crowd."

"Ah but the pickpockets and con men are hardly likely to bother you," laughed Conor.

"Rather cluttered," commented Sean as he observed a myriad of posters and screens advertising this and that. There were also places set up for outdoor dining and refreshments, people dressed up in costumes like Spider Man and all in all it was a busy and noisy environment. In some ways the chatter of loud American voices reminded him of the Shankill Pub in Belfast when they first entered to plant the bomb. Except here there was a noticeable police presence and a police station.

"Would you like to sign up for the army?" joked Conor as they passed a recruitment station. "A one-way ticket to Ukraine?"
"Sacrifice my life so the American military complex can get richer? I don't think so," replied Sean. "I understand that when they come back wounded nobody wants to know them."

They continued along the square with Sean observing the crowds of people, flashing screens and other features characterising American materialism. Occasionally an open-top double-decker bus loaded with tourists would pass by.

"There's a couple of policemen looking over in our direction," Sean commented, looking a little worried.

"Probably because you started staring at them first," retorted Conor. "In America it's not wise to stare at policemen or before you know it they'll be over checking you out. Believe me you do not want to mess with the NYPD." Connor increased his pace to put distance between the policemen and them. He encouraged Sean to do likewise now he had attracted their attention.

"How about a Covid test?" joked Conor as further into the square they passed a tent-like structure offering tests.

"Don't get me started, I've seen more than enough of that," replied Sean. "To think that in a so-called democracy we had vaccinations made mandatory."

"I think we should find an Irish pub for a Guinness," suggested Conor. "This is America, they have everything."

"Tea?" quizzed Sean.

"Well, maybe that's a bit harder to find here," laughed Conor. "They never ever forgave King George for taxing their tea."

"The black stuff will do me just fine." Sean found a seat at an empty table while Conor attracted the attention of a waiter.

"Well, what do you think of America so far?" Conor asked.

"It's certainly big, busy and noisy," replied Sean. "Not at all what I've been used to in Ireland and New Zealand."

"Indeed, it was a big shock for me too when I came to America as a youngster. We were all overwhelmed by the size of this country but in those days it seemed much safer. I might have felt more secure had my dad been with us. I was very close to him over the short time I knew him," added Conor.

"Your parents split up?" Sean asked.

"Da was imprisoned like many others fighting in the IRA. He was a hero," said Conor. "It makes me very angry just thinking about it."

"Sorry," said Sean, "they were indeed troubling times. My father was also a hero and in the IRA."

The two finished their Guinness then continued on through Times Square towards Central Park. On the way Sean commented on various buildings which caught his interest.

"Central park is very long and thin," commented Conor, as they approached the park. "We've already done quite a bit of walking today so my suggestion is we take the quickest route from one end to the other and then get a bus back. Maybe we can come back another day and see another interesting area like the Rambles."

"The Rambles?" Sean looked perplexed.

"It's a beautiful area of forestation but definitely not one to walk through at night," explained Conor.

"Oh! Is Central Park dangerous then?" Sean seemed nervous, especially given that anyone could own a gun and he had noticed many homeless destitute people already since he'd been in New York.

"Oh yes, especially the Rambles at night," replied Conor. "There have been a lot of crimes committed in Central Park even though the paths are well lit."

"Does anybody live in the park?" asked Sean. "You know, like homeless people?"

"No one is supposed to be in the park between 1 am and 6 am but that doesn't stop people." Conor laughed. "There are plenty of trees and boulders to hide behind and bushes to get lost in. They reckon there could be over one hundred homeless people living here."

"Really?" Sean looked surprised. "We're lucky to see only one or two in Christchurch."

"Just remember there are nineteen million people in the Big Apple so that doesn't seem that many really." Conor pointed to the Zoo as they walked past. "When we reach the Museum in about half an hour we will be about half way."

Sean nodded and was just pleased that at his age he was fit and healthy and enjoyed long walks.

"This is very tranquil, and aesthetically appealing," said Sean. "I could pitch a tent and happily live here. It's somewhat a contradistinction to Times Square." Sean stopped to watch a playful squirrel chewing a nut. "You don't see these cute little fellers in New Zealand."

"You didn't like Times Square then?" asked Conor.

"The jury is out on that one," laughed Sean. "Central Park is so peaceful and natural and has a relaxed, calming feeling. I think if I was homeless I'd make it my home."

"It didn't used to have lakes and vegetation, it was largely all solid rock, the rock Manhattan is built upon. They removed most of it with leftover gunpowder from the battle of Gettysburg." Conor pointed to remaining outcrops of the rock.

"The American Civil War?" suggested Sean

"Correct, Gettysburg is in Pennsylvania. Now we can't do this walk without going down Literary Walk. It acknowledges famous writers like William Shakespeare, Robert Burns, Walter Scott and perhaps, one day, yourself," teased Conor.

"Sure," joked Sean. "Do you think I'd get away with scratching my name just on a tree or a rock? It might be the closest I get to being included."

Conor laughed. "Perhaps not yet."

"I hope your boss likes my manuscript," added Sean.

"I'm sure he will," replied Conor.

"Conor, I haven't seen any homeless people here in Central Park yet," Sean said, changing the subject.

"Oh, they'll be off scavenging in the trash bins. Americans love their food and can be very wasteful. Their eyes are bigger than their stomachs and there's plenty of free stuff thrown away if you don't mind second-hand goods," laughed Conor. "Obesity is now a huge problem in America and the American health system is struggling to cope. Then there are the free newspapers, often as good as new. People buy them, read them on the bus or train or in the park, then leave them on seats or throw them away. We live in a materialistic society where we generate a lot of waste."

"Today's news, tomorrow's fish'n'chip paper," Sean remarked and they both laughed.

"That was a good walk," said Sean, as they left Central Park. "My calf muscles may have something to talk about tonight."

"You have two of them, so it could be a long conversation," laughed Conor.

Sean noticed a couple more policemen looking in their direction just as Conor spotted a bus going back in the direction of the hotel. The policemen started walking over towards them just as Conor and Sean boarded the bus.

"Maybe, I'm paranoid," declared Sean, "but I'm sure those policemen were interested in us."

"You're paranoid," laughed Conor "or maybe you just have a guilt complex," he added. "Do you have any regrets about Belfast? Would you change anything if you could?"

"Now why would I want to do that?" asked Sean. "I have no regrets."

This time they travelled for some time on the bus before disembarking. From there they walked a couple of streets and took another bus.

"I think we left just in time to avoid peak traffic," Conor commented as there was still standing room on the bus. "Tomorrow we'll visit the Statue of Liberty and some other attractions," he announced.

"This is all very nice but when do you think your boss will see me about my book?" asked Sean.

"Oh, it's early days," replied Conor. "He's currently out of town and won't be back for several days. Just enjoy the scenery meanwhile."

"Oh, I will," replied Sean. "It's been quite a change from being cooped up in my little house and never going anywhere. Father Ted thinks I'm a recluse."

"Do you see much of the Father?" asked Conor.

"Ha, that holy Joe, he often comes in unannounced and makes himself at home," laughed Sean. "Though it's nice to have a cup of tea waiting for me on the table. He's very concerned, not only about my hydration but also my soul you know, since he cannot recall me ever going to confession."

"And have you?" asked Connor as they stepped off the bus.

"Are you kidding?" laughed Sean. "Now why would I do that when I've nothing to confess?"

They walked in silence for the remaining short distance to the hotel where they parted.

Chapter Nineteen

"It's frightful that people who are so ignorant should have so much influence."

George Orwell

"Howya?"

The next morning Sean looked up from the newspaper. Conor had arrived a little bit earlier than he had expected.

"This is very worrying," said Sean.

"What's that?" asked Conor.

"The paper says that a hit man from the Middle East, the Mole Viper, has been sighted in New York. Are you sure that it's going to be safe wandering the streets with a sniper on the loose?" Sean looked concerned.

Conor laughed. "Terrorists, violent groups like ANTIFA, MS13 and many others are endemic in the USA. In fact, the Big Apple once had a Mafia problem but during the 1980s and 1990s Mayor Giuliani broke their hold, sending many to prison. Since then we have seen the return of crime. A hit man makes a good news story, sells newspapers but is nothing unusual. New York is as safe as it will ever be."

"Then it's safe to walk the streets? There are a lot of tall buildings and a sniper could be perched up there on one of the roofs," suggested Sean.

Conor laughed again. "Maybe, keep that thought for another fiction novel. These days it's never safe, Sean, but as long as you keep wearing those clothes I gave you then you shouldn't need to be worried about pick-pockets and muggers. Those are the people who you need to be worried about. It surprises me that a well-read person like you has never heard of the Mole Viper, an international assassin. It's not the first time he's been sighted in America, though he always manages to elude the authorities."

"Who do you think is his target this time?" asked Sean.

"It's hard to say," replied Conor, "but this cold-blooded killer is more than likely an assassin hired by a country like Iran to take out some politician or business leader. Interpol has pursued him for decades but every time he has proven elusive."

"It seems that New York seems to attract them all, you know the mafia, the twin towers and now this," Sean commented.

"As I said we've nineteen million people and that makes us a good target for those who have a score to settle with America. Our meddling in other countries' politics and the destruction we've caused in wars we've started overseas have made many enemies," replied Conor. "What's the latest with Ukraine?"

"Oh the USA have their 101 Airborne practicing war drills on the Ukraine border," informed Sean. "Now that's not a good sign."

"That figures." Conor looked disgusted. "They're playing with fire and just one wrong move and it's Armageddon."

"Indeed," replied Sean. "Your politicians seem to have a false sense of invincibility. They've already drained US oil reserves to keep prices down during the midterm election; as well as having substantially reduced the American arsenal supplying weapons to Ukraine. Not a good situation if they end up in war with Russia, and what now if China chooses to attack Taiwan?"

"Well, let's leg it and find a diner. I think a sandwich or two and a Guinness would go down nicely."

"Agreed, I could murder a couple of jars of the black stuff." Sean looked quite pleased to put aside the media spreading doom and gloom for something positive and exciting.

"Today I will take you first to see the Empire State Building and then we'll visit the Statue of Liberty," said Conor.

"Great," replied Sean as they set off to find a restaurant.

After they had eaten, they took a bus and walked the remaining few hundred metres to the Empire State Building.

"So when was this building built?" asked Sean. "I know that it's been around for some time."

"Nineteen thirty," replied Conor. "Isn't it amazing for its age? Would you like to go up to the viewing area on top? You have to pay."

Sean shook his head, looking at the queue. "You might find it hard to believe but I've never been up a tall building in my life and after the Christchurch earthquake I don't have any desire to."

"Over one hundred floors in the Empire State Building," said Conor.

"Amazing." Sean looked in awe. "To think way back then they were able to build something that big and it must have been during the Great Depression."

"Perhaps that was why it was built then, to provide jobs for the many unemployed," suggested Conor. "I guess there aren't many tall buildings in Belfast and I expect Christchurch is the same."

"There were more tall buildings in Christchurch before the earthquake," replied Sean, "but many had to come down due to earthquake damage. There are many skyscrapers in Sydney but I never went up any."

"Well, we best be heading to the Staten Ferry. That's where you'll get the best view of the Statue of Liberty if you don't like queues and heights." Conor started to walk away from the Empire State Building down the sidewalk and Sean followed.

"Sorry, did you say that you lived in Sydney as well?" asked Conor.

"That was until my dad died," Sean replied.

"So you left Ireland for Sydney?" asked Conor.

"Correct," replied Sean.

"How did you manage that if your dad was in the IRA and had a criminal record? I thought Australian immigration was very selective."

"He didn't have one," said Sean.

"He didn't?" Conor looked puzzled. "Then your family moved to New Zealand?"

"Just me and my Mum, but after she died in Auckland I moved to Christchurch," explained Sean.

"Now you're on your own?" Conor asked. "No other family?"

"Correct, just me but it's much easier that way."

"And you Conor, do you have a wife and family?"

"It was very hard for us after we left Ireland and my mother struggled having to raise nine children, one a baby, all on her own with very little money for many years," explained Conor, looking very upset. "But at least we were safe in America away from those who wanted us dead."

"Oh! You too?" Sean looked surprised.

"At first we settled in Boston. It's a very Irish city with the Irish being the largest ethnic group there. However, as we found out, it wasn't just Irish Catholics immigrating to escape poverty and violence. There were also Protestant thugs like some members of the Shankill Butchers who had taken refuge."

"Not here in America?" Sean looked worried. "I thought they were all rounded up and incarcerated. Surely, they'd all be dead and gone or incapacitated by now, wouldn't they?"

"Only some were imprisoned," said Conor. "As you know we lived in an unfair society where there was one set of rules for the loyalists and another for the republicans. So as a family, for our own safety, we moved to New York. Being such a big city we could quite easily disappear here."

"Good move," said Sean.

"I didn't settle down until well into my thirties, having experienced so much trauma and having to help support my poor mother and family. Over those few years she aged quickly from being a beautiful young lady to looking like an elderly grey-haired lady. She never really got to enjoy the grand lifestyle America offered and died young. When I did marry, it only lasted ten years after my wife found a younger man. I was left on my own. My wife explained that she couldn't live with both me and the baggage from my past. My life has been hell. It makes me very angry just reflecting on the past." Conor pointed to another very tall building.

"I was married once but we didn't have children," said Sean.

"So what do you do as a single man?" asked Conor.

"I fix computers, write novels and basically keep to myself," laughed Sean.

"No clubs, women in your life or drinking mates?" enquired Conor.

"Correct! The Father calls me a recluse and he was ecstatic when I told him about going to America."

Conor spotted a bus that would shorten their journey and they jumped on board.

"Mohammed busy again?" asked Sean. "I haven't seen him for a few days."

"He's in Washington with the boss," replied Conor. "But they'll both be back in a couple of days."

Sean followed Conor off the bus and they walked the remaining distance to the pier where the Staten Island Ferry departed.

"You needn't worry, the ferry is free," informed Conor who had concluded that Sean was frugal. "The ferry passes close to the Statue of Liberty but at a fast speed so we need to make sure we choose our seating wisely for the best view. Of course we'll get to see it on the way back as well."

Conor and Sean boarded the ferry and shortly after the boat was full and on its way.

"I'm told that the statue was built to commemorate the abolition of slavery and to honour French and US relations," informed Conor

"Slavery was a big thing in America from what I've heard," commented Sean.

"You might not believe it," added Conor, "but the statute was built in Paris and shipped in crates to America. Gustave Eiffel helped to build it."

"French? I thought it looked Italian," commented Sean as the boat passed by the 151 foot structure. "Was that Gustave Eiffel of the Eiffel tower?"

"Bang on," replied Conor. "They say it is supposed to be a Roman Goddess. At one stage it was the tallest building in America. Over three hundred steps to the crown so I don't think you'd want to go up there."

"Far too high for me," laughed Sean, as the boat had now passed the statute and was headed towards Staten Island.

"In the distance you can see the Brooklyn Bridge," said Conor, pointing up the river.

"Wasn't that the first bridge to use steel for cable wire," asked Sean.

"Correct. It was brilliant nineteenth century engineering," confirmed Conor

"So what is there to see on Staten Island?" asked Sean as the boat pulled alongside the pier.

"Heaps," replied Conor, "but I thought you'd like to visit Our Lady of Mount Carmel Grotto."

"A bit late to attend mass," laughed Sean. "Maybe confession — just joking!"

"Not a bad idea," retorted Conor. "It might be a good time to get yourself right with God at least."

"What do you mean?"

"Well, a lot of bad things happened in Northern Ireland though confession is not going to stop people seeking revenge," explained Conor.

"I have no worries. I did nothing," lied Sean, "and besides most of those people around back then are now too old or incapacitated."

"I'd like to think so too," replied Conor "but the hurt is passed down many generations and the past is bound to catch up with you sooner or later."

The two found their way to the church and both knelt before the altar. After that they visited the botanic gardens, an art gallery and a museum to fill in the thirty minutes between ferries.

"Staten Island has more people than your city of Christchurch," informed Conor.

"Really?" replied Sean, as the two made their way back to the ferry.

"And it has an important Irish connection through the Earl of Limerick, Thomas Dongan, who served as the Governor of New York during the seventeenth century. He was the one who included Staten Island as a county of New York."

"That's amazing, you know your history," replied Sean, who had found an ideal seat for viewing the Statue of Liberty on the return trip. "To think that the Irish have had such a big part to play in American history."

"So where do you think the American Constitution is kept?" quizzed Conor.

"Ah, I know the answer to that. I saw it on TV. It's in the National Museum," replied Sean.

"But you didn't know that there was a copy kept under the Statue of Liberty did you?"

"Is there? Indeed I didn't," replied Sean as they sped past the statue.

"Well," said Sean, feeling quite pleased with the afternoon's outing as they left the ferry, "this time I didn't have any policemen staring at me."

"There you go." Conor spotted a bus and they ran to catch it.

"But," added Sean, out of breath, "I never looked to see."

"Very wise, if they think you have a gun they shoot first, Sean."

"And ask questions later," added Sean.

"No Sean, they shoot to kill. A dead body can't talk," chuckled Conor.

"Saving paperwork," suggested Sean.

"More a case of shooting first. A lot of policemen get shot in this country," explained Conor.

Nearer to the hotel they left the bus and walked the rest of the way.

"I think my highlights to date have been the boat ride today and Central Park," concluded Sean.

Chapter Twenty

"Ye cannot see the wood for the trees."

John Heywood

Sean was up earlier the next morning so he'd have more time to browse through the newspapers. Over the last few mornings he had decided to branch out from his traditional bagel breakfast and try the continental and fried breakfast options. During breakfast he got to talk to another Irish man who had come to live in America. The man told him that his family had originally moved to Scotland for a better life and a job. It seemed that the Irish uprisings had impacted on many migrating to other parts of the world.

Later Sean returned to the lobby. He found his favourite armchair and started to read through the day's news. Near midday he felt a tap on his shoulder. It was Conor.

"So what's in the headlines today?" he asked.

"Oh," replied Sean. "We're lucky to be alive. The Mole Viper was sighted at Staten Island."

"Now that's hard to believe," replied Conor. "What would he be doing there?"

"Well, that's what's been reported," said Sean.

"So are you coming or do you want to fill your head with fake news?" asked Conor. "Today we're eating at the café next to one of the pathways leading into the Rambles at Central Park."

"Great," replied Sean. "I was eager to visit this famous Rambles. A man at breakfast told me that there are over two hundred bird species there."

"There probably is, there are a lot of trees and shrubs, though I haven't seen many birds there myself but it does cover thirty seven acres. In a big concrete jungle like New York, Central Park, particularly the Rambles, is an area to escape to. Now we're going to take several buses to 77th Street where we will start our journey," said Conor.

"Mohammed is still busy then?" probed Sean, as the bus pulled alongside them at the stop.

"Especially today. He's with the boss all day," replied Conor as he stepped onto the bus.

"Never mind," replied Sean, "another day sightseeing and there's so much more to see from being elevated in a bus."

After changing buses, it wasn't long before they reached the 77th Street entrance to Central Park and the café Conor had chosen.

"So you were telling me that your dad was in prison," probed Sean.

"Yes at the Maze, the same place as Bobby Sands, the leader of the IRA," replied Conor.

"An interesting character," commented Sean. "How did Sands come to join the IRA?"

"Like most of us he had a pretty rough childhood and had been assaulted a number of times by Protestant gangs. He joined in 1972 and was imprisoned several times on weapon possession."

"Just on weapon possession? Pathetic," commented Sean.

"And Sands was young, only twenty seven when he died," added Conor.

"A real shame they allowed him to starve himself to death when he would have done so much more as a politician," commented Sean.

"Oh, he achieved quite a lot through his hunger strike and death," replied Conor. "It was a terrifying experience for anyone incarcerated at the Maze with Protestant psychopaths also as inmates. But it was the prison officers who were the worst, most of whom were loyalists. My father said that the most terrifying part was when his cell door was opened. He would be dragged out naked and beaten to a pulp before being thrown back into the cells. He went through hell and so did our family. No wonder he died shortly after being released."

"The hunger strike, what was that about?" asked Sean, biting into a cheese and ham sandwich.

"What was that about?" Conor looked angrily at Sean. "Pity you never experienced their conditions and showed some empathy." Conor paused to sip his coffee and regain his composure. "Holy Mother of God, what was it all about?" he repeated angrily. "It was terrible! How would you like to be locked up in a cell with only a chamber pot and no shower and toilet?"

"I have for a number of days," replied Sean.

"I'm not talking police cells," barked Conor. "This is the real thing where people are sent to spend the rest of their lives. How would you like it if every time you needed to leave your cell you got beaten up?"

"My experience was just a police cell," conceded Sean, "but it was still most unpleasant."

"Then," continued Conor, "they were treated like criminals having to wear prison uniforms. So many, like my dad, refused and instead wrapped themselves in a blanket while others went naked. The situation worsened with the dirty protest."

"What was that?" asked Sean.

"You told me you were IRA and you don't know?" scoffed Conor. "It was a protest over the conditions. The IRA inmates refused to leave their cells and emptied their chamber pots in the cell and smeared excrement on the walls to spread maggots."

"Gross," replied Sean, remembering the putrid smell of urine he had experienced. "Given these horrific conditions, did any prisoners try to escape?"

"Now that's an interesting question," said Conor, finishing his coffee and becoming more relaxed. "There was one big breakout in 1983. I remember that because my dad almost died from one of the beatings he received at the time. We could do nothing as we'd have been murdered had we returned to Ireland. Apparently, thirty-eight prisoners grabbed a prison lorry and broke out. On another occasion a twelve metre tunnel was dug but that was discovered. Haha, then there was one prisoner who dressed as a woman and was never captured."

"Now that's quite ingenious," laughed Sean. "It's amazing that a prisoner, presumably unshaven and unkempt in appearance, could pass off as a woman. I wonder how he managed that?"

Conor rose from the table. "Well if we're going to walk The Rambles then we best be off."

At the back of the café was a track through the trees which they followed until it joined a more official track.

"The walk is about two and a half miles," said Conor. "That's one way, so five miles returning a different path."

They followed the track through the bush to the boathouse and lake and found a bench to rest and to enjoy the scenery and tranquillity.

"As you can see there are many tracks, lots of benches and off track places like this lake," said Conor.

"Is he homeless?" asked Sean, pointing to an elderly man feeding the ducks. The elderly man stood at the lake's edge, throwing bread crumbs to the ducks. His long grey shoulder length hair looked knotted and matted and the shirt hanging from his shoulders looked moth eaten and a size or two too big. Even his trousers looked to have seen better days with windows for his knees to gape through.

"Possibly," replied Conor, "but the homeless are usually jobless people of a working age. There are a lot of them since the economy took a downturn. It's quite surprising seeing someone so old here who's not in care though. Most of the homeless would be hanging around food outlets in town and begging for money I would've thought."

They continued along the track, passing a number of people also out for a walk. The Rambles seemed to be a popular spot.

"This stream runs all around Central Park," said Conor as they crossed over a bridge. "So you like this better than Times Square?"

"Times Square is very cluttered and man-made, whereas Central Park is very natural," replied Sean.

"What if I told you that Central Park was man-made: the lake, stream, cascade waterfall and probably even the big rock in the middle of the lake where turtles sit," laughed Conor.

"Really?" Sean looked surprised.

"You may also be surprised to know that part of it was Seneca Village which was occupied by African American and Irish people," informed Conor. "It was settled by the Irish in the nineteenth century after The Great Famine."

"Irish?" Sean again looked surprised.

"But they were evicted, though compensated when it was decided New York needed a green space," added Conor. "There are still some remains of the Irish village."

"Irish? No wonder I feel at home here," joked Sean.

"Now if we go down there that track takes us to 79th Street and the Stone Arch entrance." Conor pointed to his left. "So let's go and have a look at the Stone Arch," Conor said, noticing two policemen walking down the track towards them.

"So what was your experience as a child growing up in Northern Ireland? Was it anything like Bobby Sands?" asked Sean.

"Probably much of a muchness being bullied but unlike Sands I grew up in Derry."

"Not Belfast then?" Sean looked perplexed.

"My father was involved in the DCDA set up because Catholics were concerned over the Unionists gerrymandering city elections," explained Conor.

"Sorry, DCDA? What's that?" asked Sean.

The Derry Citizen's Defense Association." Conor looked back to see if the policemen had followed but they hadn't.

"It was the DCDA who were instrumental in bringing about the battle of Bogside in 1969 between the Republicans and Loyalists; three days of rioting. The government had to bring in the army to control the situation," said Conor.

"Were you involved in the riots?" asked Sean.

"Hardly, I was just a babe," replied Conor, "but my father told me all about them. Anyhow, the government got smart and tried to infiltrate the DCDA by planting moles. That's when we moved to Belfast."

"For safety reasons?" suggested Sean.

"My dad knew too much. He was in it far too deep. This is the Stone Arch and through it is 79th Street," said Conor. "Now let's return back to the track we were following."

They continued to follow various tracks, some going up-hill and others crossing rustic bridges. After a time, Conor pointed out that they were now on the return journey.

"I could do this again," replied Sean as they finally reached the exit and headed back to the hotel.

Chapter Twenty-one

"If you want the present to be different from the past, study the past."

Baruch Spinoza

Conor was late arriving the next day and didn't look at all pleased. On his shoulder he carried a bag. He didn't greet Sean with a howya this time, instead he reached into his bag and pulled out the manuscript.

"Here," he said, passing the manuscript to Sean. "Keep this because the boss still needs it. He's now read through it and wasn't at all happy."

"Oh," said Sean. "Do you know what areas in particular?"

"He said a lot of it was rubbish. I know for one thing that he didn't like you denigrating the Iranians," replied Conor. "Holy Mother of God, the Americans do it all the time without this as well."

"I can make changes," replied Sean, putting down the newspaper. "It's just a manuscript and all is negotiable."

"Well, you tell that to the boss. Good luck, you'll need it," mocked Conor.

Sean, somewhat upset, returned the manuscript to his room, placing it on the table before rejoining Conor in the lobby.

"Anyhow, what is there to report today? More one-sided fake news I imagine," Conor said somewhat scathingly. "That's all we get these days from the media. It's all rubbish."

"Glad you asked." Sean's eyes lit up. "We now know the Mole Viper's targets and it's satisfying to know that he wasn't in New York."

"What do you mean?" probed Conor. "Of course he was. There have been sightings all week."

"Well, according to the paper he was in Washington all the time and shot two Republican senators while they were playing golf. They believe that it might be a reprisal for killing General Soleimani who the Trump administration had killed. These two senators were also the ones bringing evidence before the senate on Iran developing nuclear weapons."

"Were they killed?" asked Conor.

"The paper doesn't say. All it says is that they were rushed off to hospital."

"Rubbish, of course they've been killed. The Mole Viper has never been known to miss," informed Conor who seemed in a foul mood. "So I take it that it's safe to go out to Times Square then and check out some shops after we grab a bite to eat or are you once again going to be paranoid?" snapped Conor.

"Indeed, this time it looks to be safe with the Mole Viper having achieved his mission. He's probably somewhere back in the Middle East now, sitting outside in the sunshine enjoying a beer. I'd love to know what your boss didn't like in my story," added Sean, still chewing over Conor's earlier comment.

"Exactly, he's hardly likely to be in Times Square," chuckled Conor. "Not on the doorstep of the trigger-happy NYPD. Now that would be suicide. It would only take them minutes to close off the area and have it swarming with trigger-happy police. He'd be dead meat in no time."

The two set off for a diner to have a sandwich or two and coffee, this time in Times Square. Sean would have preferred tea had it been on offer. Conor really didn't mind as he'd got used to drinking coffee.

Times Square was as Sean had remembered it, bustling with tourists, many probably from other American States. The place, with its flashing screens, was buzzing with activity as they approached one of the areas near where the streets crossed and open-top tourist buses rolled through. As usual, the place was noisy and there were police everywhere but Sean had learned not to catch their attention. They found a seat outside and had some lunch.

"This will be the last day you'll see me," divulged Conor as they stood up following lunch.

"Oh! That's a shame," replied Sean. "Well I certainly appreciate having been shown all the attractions while waiting to see the boss. It was nice to have a fellow countryman showing me around and the occasional drink or two."

"Not my choice at all," barked Conor as he walked towards the crossing. "It was a job that had to be done but at least Times Square brings back some happy memories. It was quite meaningful for me after we moved to New York with all its theatres, museums and restaurants…"

"And bars," added Sean. "I could murder a Guinness right now."

"And I could murder you," snapped Conor. "After what you and your father did to my family."

"Sorry! What?" Sean froze and looked at Conor in disbelief. "What do you mean? What are you talking about?"

"I'm the son of Liam O'Mahony," said Conor, reaching into his bag. "And I've lived for this moment."

"Liam O'Mahony?" Sean looked puzzled. "Who's that?"

"Holy Mother of God, you know very well who I mean!" roared Conor. "The man who you and your dad betrayed and sent to his death. All the misery you and your dad caused for our family. The mob torched our house and our family were always living in fear, even after coming to America. None of us ever managed to live a normal life. One of my sisters ended up committing suicide. You have a lot to answer for."

"I was just a boyo at the time and did what I was told," explained Sean. "It was your dad and mine who carried out the bombing. I was just a lad, only thirteen at the time."

"Liar!" snarled Conor. "Your Dad helped you but you were the brains behind making the bombs. Da described you as cold blooded and evil, a psychopath. He had even witnessed you taking a shot at a policeman. You were no better than the Shankill Butchers and you've even told me this week that you're not at all remorseful. As for your dad being a hero, you both set my dad up to take the fall. Your dads a traitor and no hero. Da was loyal to the IRA until the end."

"That's not true," quivered Sean, "and my dad was a hero and helped to win the war against Germany."

"That's right, a traitor who sided with the English and was still working for them," snarled Conor. "Da suspected there were moles in the organisation but he made one mistake: trusting you and your dad, not realising that you were the moles working for British Intelligence. Your dad was a traitor, not a hero."

"That's not true at all - we were both loyal to the cause," argued Sean. "We were soldiers and we put our necks on the line for the IRA. It was not the first bombing we'd carried out."

"Then why didn't you both go to prison after being arrested?" pressed Conor. "I bet you can't explain that, can you? Why did you let my dad take the rap?"

"Do you think they'd want bomb-makers in a prison teaching others the skill?" replied Sean.

"Rubbish! That's not convincing," barked Conor. "Probably the best and most successful bomb-maker, Shane O'Doherty, was sent to prison. Sorry, your explanation doesn't wash."

"Sending a war hero to prison would destroy the British narrative that the IRA was just a band of thugs," Sean continued. "If people saw that the IRA included everyday Irish men and women, including war heroes, then it could be politically damaging and even bring world condemnation. Now the authorities wouldn't want that."

"Bollocks! Not convincing. Just because your dad dropped a handful of bombs on defenceless women and children in Germany, it doesn't make him a war hero," mocked Conor. "You were moles, traitors to the cause and you destroyed my family. The last I ever saw of my father was in prison. When he did get out, they wouldn't let him into America because of his criminal record."

"It happened to many. He was like my father, a soldier fighting a cause. Do you think I never suffered?" asked Sean. "It wasn't nice leaving family and friends without even a goodbye, or to have my father and mother murdered by the Shankill Butchers."

Mohammed pulled up on a motorbike and sat there waiting. What were Conor's intentions?

"Murdered? They were murdered?" For a moment Conor hesitated before reaching into his bag and presenting a revolver. "This is your day of reckoning but I'm not going to shoot you. I couldn't even kill a fly. I've waited a long time for this day, for revenge."

"There's no need for this. We've all suffered enough already and we were on the same side," pleaded Sean.

 Conor raised the gun, firing it twice into the air then thrusting it into Sean's hand.

"Goodbye and good riddance," shouted Conor as he stormed off, jumping on the back of Mohammed's motorbike.

 Sean stood there dumbfounded, holding the gun while watching Conor and Mohammed speed away. Sean looked around at his predicament. People were running for cover in all directions and he was now the perceived villain.

Somebody shouted "It's the Mole Viper," amongst the screams and shouts. Down the Central Park end of Times Square he could see policemen running towards him with their guns drawn and he knew that gun or no gun they would shoot to kill. He removed his jacket and hung it over his arm to conceal the gun as he ran through Times Square from the police. Surely they wouldn't try and hit him from a distance with the risk of taking out an innocent bystander. His best option was to move into a more crowded area to get lost amongst the crowd. Much further down the square he was able to do just this as the people there were oblivious to what had recently taken place. He moved briskly through the crowds with the intention of leaving Times Square before the NYPD had it blocked off. As he passed by a group of young women, he heard one, who had just been on her mobile, telling her friend "We need to get out of here, the Mole Viper is here in Times Square."

He spotted a bus just ahead and grabbed the opportunity to jump on, not knowing where it was heading as long as it took him far away from Times Square. Out of the window he watched as a number of policemen ran towards the Square. If they seriously believed that it was the Mole Viper then the whole of New York could be on high alert and a hive of police activity.

Five stops later Sean spotted a bus heading in the opposite direction going towards Central Park. He left his bus and boarded the other bus travelling in the opposite direction. Central Park seemed his best option with plenty of places where he could hide until dusk at least. With the NYPD and probably FBI everywhere, it would be far too risky trying to get back to his hotel. As he travelled back past Times Square he could see flashing lights as police cars descended onto the area from everywhere. It was amusing to think that the NYPD believed he was still there. He had escaped just in time and they wouldn't be expecting him to be going back in the opposite direction now. When the bus drew very close to Central Park, he disembarked and made the rest of the way on foot. Fortunately, he didn't see any policemen or police vehicles on the way. He felt confident that for now he was safe, believing that nobody had seen him enter the park. He made his way through the park towards the Rambles where he could hide out until dusk. There were plenty of trees to hide behind and even in other areas he could hide behind shrubs and rocks.

He worked his way towards the Rambles, casually admiring the attractions like any other tourist. There were small groups of people walking through the park and he did not want to draw attention. How would the characters in my books react in such a situation?, he thought. His answer: cool, calm and collected. He searched one of the rubbish bins and found a newspaper. In a more secluded part of the park he found a bench and sat there reading it, hoping the remaining hours before dusk would pass quickly. It worked as few people passed by and he could have been a garden gnome to those who did.

It was now starting to get quite dark when he left to find a private place amongst the bushes in the absence of a nearby toilet. Now somewhat more comfortable, he was returning to the bench when he noticed a homeless man had occupied part of it. It was the same elderly man he and Conor had observed the previous day. Startled by Sean's appearance, the elderly man looked up from the newspaper he was reading and stared in Sean's direction. At the same time, Sean heard voices and could make out two Central Park policemen approaching, both carrying torches. He quickly retreated into the bush while the two policemen passed by. That was the first patrol he had seen and he was sure that there would be more as dusk approached. Sean returned to the bench, joining the homeless man who kindly offered him half of the newspaper to read. This was a new experience for Sean as he sat there speechless next to him. Perhaps at one time this man had been somebody important, a husband or father and maybe once wealthy. Now his neglected long, straggly, greasy, grey hair and unkempt appearance were the signs of hard times.

Sean sat there in discomfort and re-read several newspaper articles with the assistance of the bright path lamp. Suddenly he saw lights and heard voices. Were the policemen coming back? He was rising to return to the bush when the old man grabbed him firmly by the arm and held him down.

"Here," he said and passed him a well-worn and torn jacket and an old cap to wear, plus a moth-eaten blanket to throw over his trousers. "They'll give you no trouble." Now he himself felt and looked just like a homeless man. The old man wrapped his arm around Sean just as the policemen appeared. They shone their torches for a second at the two men on the bench before continuing on their patrol.

Chapter Twenty-two

"Like branches on a tree, our lives may grow in different directions, yet our roots remain as one."

Suzy Kassem

"Well now, that was close, Sean," laughed the homeless man in an Irish voice.

"Sorry?" Sean stood there confused and speechless but thankful as he looked into the old man's parched, wrinkled and unshaven face. He had kind searching, blue eyes that looked warm and friendly. It was strange for an elderly man to be roughing it in Central Park.

"You don't recognise me, Sean?" enquired the elderly man.

Sean looked again at the elderly man's face. Behind the pale, wrinkled complexion and dishevelled appearance there was something vaguely familiar but surely there was absolutely no way that it could be.

"I know that I'm now very old but don't you recognise your own father?"

"Da?" Sean looked stunned. His heart began to pound and tears of joy streamed from his eyes. "Is that really you? I don't understand it. Is it really you? Oh, Da!" Sean reached across to embrace his father and in that moment all his anxiety subsided and nothing mattered more than being reunited with him.

"Well, it can't be anyone else. I know that it's surprising I'm still alive and kicking at my age," laughed Danny, pulling his son towards him and giving him a big hug. "I've always been jammy. Oh dear! I see you've got yourself into some strife carrying a gun. Now would it have to have something to do with Ireland, my son?"

"It does, Da," replied Sean, finally letting go of his father. "Remember Liam O'Mahony who assisted us in the Shankill bombing?"

"Do I ever," recalled Danny. "It was terrible what happened to him and his family. I wish I could've changed everything. They suffered so badly but we didn't know at the time."

"Well, his son Conor tricked me into coming to America so he could get his revenge. I now have the NYPD out in full force looking for me. They're convinced I'm the assassin they call the Mole Viper."

"Oh yes, the Mole Viper. I recall reading about him," replied Danny. "I might be homeless but I still get my papers delivered in my letterbox most days."

"Letter box?" Sean looked confused.

Danny pointed to the trash can. "I also get meals delivered some days," he laughed.

"So Liam's family is here in New York? Now that's interesting. How long have they been here?"

"Since the bombing, you need not worry Da. Up until now, everyone thought you were dead," said Sean. "Colleen will be so pleased, as I am, to know you were never brutally murdered. She will be even more excited to see you in person."

"At my age I'm not worried about Conor or anyone else seeking revenge," replied Danny. "I've made my peace with God. It was a terrible thing we did, that bombing, and Conor has every right to wish me dead for leaving his dad to take the rap. If he finds me then so be it. I've lived a long and happy life."

"What we did was right, Da. The Shankill gang deserved to be blown to smithereens," Sean replied. "They were monsters. I have absolutely no regrets."

"No-one but God has the right to take a life," replied Danny. "It was wrong."

"And the bombing over Germany, was that any different?" asked Sean.

"Hitler had to be stopped and when you're dropping bombs you don't witness the misery and destruction that you've caused. It's still wrong to take a life regardless. It seemed that after I sought God's forgiveness that the Shankill Butchers ceased to pursue me." Danny put his arm around Sean and gave him another hug. "Oh, it's so good to see you. You're no longer my little boy. What a delightful surprise. The Virgin Mary is certainly watching over me. She has been ever since I came to New York."

"Now tell me about your Mum and Colleen," requested Danny, "Then I'll share my story. Are they all well?"

"Colleen and Trev are well and you have grandchildren who are now adults," said Sean. "I've never seen them though as I live in New Zealand."

"That's nice to know that I have grandchildren," Danny smiled, "and sad that I never got to know them."

"You will, but I fear that Colleen and Trev may be getting into deeper waters," continued Sean.

"Oh!" Danny looked concerned.

"They're strongly opposed to American and Chinese interference in Australia and Trev, with my help, wants to make a pipe bomb," said Sean.

"Oh dear!" Danny looked shocked. "You mustn't get involved. And your Mum, how is she?"

Sean sobbed. "Sadly she died about four years after we settled in Auckland. She was killed in a car accident, maybe even murdered."

"Oh, how terrible." Danny wiped the tears from his eyes. "That would explain everything. But please tell me more about what has happened since I left."

They sat down and Sean spent the next hour or so updating Danny on all that had happened since Sydney. At one stage the police patrol returned but, having checked them out previously, walked straight past, not even acknowledging their presence.

"Oh, my poor Deidre. I hope she didn't suffer, though it's unlikely that she was murdered; more likely to have been an accident," replied Danny who was still upset. "It was always me the gang was after, not your mum. I'm pleased to hear that nothing has happened since and once you return to New Zealand, I don't think Conor will be any further problem now that he's taken his revenge leaving you to our trigger-happy police. With the NYPD mobilised it's best for you to spend the night here then leave for your hotel just before sunrise," advised Danny. "I can show you a shortcut back to the road."

"That's my thinking too, Da," said Sean. "What a day and I'm taking you back to New Zealand where you'll be treated like a king. You can live with me in my small house. It's what you deserve. I'm not going to lose you again, that's for sure."

"We'll see," replied Danny, wiping his eyes.

"Your story, Da?" reminded Sean. "I'm dying to hear it."

"Oh, well I guess it started one afternoon when I was returning home from work. I turned up to take the Mosman Ferry and who should be there by the wharf but Shane Gallagher, his younger version and, would you believe it, big Tommy Hegarty."

"Haha, Tommy Hegarty, that was just a lookalike, Da," laughed Sean. "I came across him a number of times down George Street in Sydney where he must work. Initially I was fooled too."

"Not this man, Sean. I know for sure this was definitely Tommy Hegarty," said Danny. "The fact that they'd discovered what ferry I was taking suggested they were close to finding where we lived. Hegarty obviously wanted part of the action."

"He did get wounded in the bombing," interrupted Sean, "and was sure to want revenge."

Danny produced another moth hole-ridden woollen blanket and wrapped it around himself. "It can get a little cold here over the winter but I can always go to the shelter when it really gets freezing. I'm not that silly to brave the snow and frosts. You needn't worry."

"You won't have to put up with that any more, Da. I'll see to that," said Sean. "This is cold, just like the police cell in Belfast but this time I don't have to put up with the putrid smell of urine. It's worth freezing to death just to be back with you."

"So my body odour isn't that bad," laughed Danny, giving Sean another hug. "I'm not sure when I last washed. But for me this has to be one of the best days in my life." Danny shed some more tears. "Oh, I have missed you, Colleen and your mum so much. Life for me has never been easy with the bombing raids over Germany, the Irish situation and having to desert my wife and family but I've survived. Despite my sinful past, the Virgin Mary has been kind and her angels have watched and guarded over me. Every day there is a treat waiting for me in a rubbish bin. For that I'm eternally grateful."

"So what happened?" asked Sean.

"Oh, well it's no different to a mother bird or any other animal trying to protect their young, they make themselves the prey drawing the predator far away from their family. I booked a plane flight to Los Angeles for the family and had the travel agent print out the flight details. I conveniently had it poking out of a jacket pocket then one afternoon after work went to take the ferry and who should be there but as expected Shane, his son and Tommy. I made sure they'd see me and I had a taxi waiting for a quick get-a-way. Shane and his son gave chase and I just happened to drop the plane flight details in the process. I also let it known to my employer and a number of others that we were off to Los Angeles. Several days later I cancelled the flights for you and your Mum and took an earlier flight to LA."

"That was the day you never returned?" suggested Sean.

"Correct. That was a very hard day for me, knowing I'd never see any of you again. I spent weeks, maybe months grieving the loss and at times I hoped it would be safe to return. I wanted to so much but each year that passed, to my disappointment, it still didn't look safe. But my plan worked and the Shankill Butchers came searching for me in LA," laughed Danny. "It was then I knew you'd be safe."

"It was pretty hard for all of us left to think you were dead, Da. They even found a body in the harbour which the police believed to be yours."

"Well, now you know it wasn't," laughed Danny.

"Fortunately we didn't view it as the police said it was so badly beaten and unrecognisable," informed Sean. "We were very shaken at the time."

"I've always been jammy and I had the backup plan for you and your Mum to move to New Zealand, which seemed to work," added Danny.

"When the gang got close to finding me in LA, I moved to New York and after that they must have given up. After you moved to Auckland, I made contact with your Mum, I had to. I couldn't leave her mourning, believing I was dead. I owed her an explanation at the very least. My being alive remained our secret to protect the family. She was not happy at the time and I got an earful. Did I ever!"

"As would be expected," laughed Sean. "Ma was never short of a few words."

"But she understood, I think, and we kept in touch," continued Danny. "We both missed each other immensely. I loved your mother," Danny wiped his eyes, "and there wasn't a day that went past without me wanting to be with her. She was planning to join me in New York but then all communication ceased."

"The car accident," suggested Sean.

"If only I'd known." Danny wiped his eyes again. "You can take all safety measures in life but when your time is up you have no control."

Another police patrol passed by and once again the officers did not check them out.

"Conor said that you were a mole working for British Intelligence," probed Sean.

"Total rubbish!" replied Danny. "I suspect the CIA was somehow involved though. I was one of just a handful in the IRA to know we had CIA involvement providing us with arms but there were no moles in our cell group to my knowledge. The Garda told me we were betrayed, something I had already suspected after the police were onto us straight after the bombing. Over the years I've given this further thought and have concluded that the IRA, or maybe the CIA, betrayed us. It makes a lot of sense why Liam, not part of our cell group, was chosen to assist us in the bombing."

"Why?" asked Sean.

"Because both Liam and I were privy to knowing about CIA involvement and we had both been fiercely opposed to this even if we were receiving firearms and materials for bomb making."

"Why's that?" asked Sean.

"CIA help doesn't come without a price, Sean. As the IRA, we were trying to rid ourselves of British dominance not to replace it with American. It was so dumb involving them," replied Danny.

"Agreed, and I'm proud of you, Da," added Sean. "You're my hero."

"They also knew that we were both religiously loyal to the cause and wouldn't talk when arrested or incarcerated," continued Danny. "But I wasn't incarcerated and remained a threat; I could expose CIA involvement and put the USA in an embarrassing position."

"You had to be silenced and they knew that the Shankill Butchers would do their dirty work," suggested Sean.

"Exactly! We had reached our best use-by date," laughed Danny. "But these days, 'best use-by date' is a very popular meal here in the park."

"That's terrible," replied Sean.

"That's politics."

"How did you come to be homeless?" asked Sean.

"I wasn't always homeless. When I came to New York I came with an excellent knowledge on computers and attained a well-paying job. However, a good portion went to pay for the rent as New York is an expensive place to live. I worked until I was seventy but by then I had well and truly burnt out in electronics. I have always kept good health but Father Kelly talked me into a Catholic aged care facility when I was 85. Father Kelly has been very good to me, providing me with clothes from the charity shop, as well as the occasional meal. He even provides me with occasional access to a shower. I didn't stay long as I preferred my independence. It wasn't the life for me, stuck in care waiting to die, so I went back to caring for myself. Even though I'd saved hard over the years, it didn't take long before my remaining savings ran out and I could no longer afford to rent. I've always loved the outdoors and Central Park and one day I got talking to a homeless man here. He would have been 97 this year but he died last year. He lived in Central Park and enjoyed it." Danny yawned and stretched out.

"But Da, at your age you shouldn't be roughing it out here."

"This is my life. In aged care I had no life," said Danny, closing his eyes. Danny lay on the bench and with a snort dropped off to sleep. Sean curled up beside him with a large smile on his face, once again reunited with his father. Today had been a miracle. Perhaps the Virgin Mary had been watching over him. Ninety-five and still alive and healthy. Colleen will never believe it. He fell asleep, comforted to know his dad hadn't been murdered.

Sean felt a tapping on his leg which started to get very bothersome. He opened his eyes to see a bright light shining in his face.

"The park closes at 1 am," said a voice.

Sean rubbed his eyes and moved to a sitting position. "My dad is ninety-five years old," whispered Sean. "He's fast asleep and in no position to move at this hour."

"We know the old guy," said one of the two policemen. "So he's your father?"

"Indeed, it's a miracle he's alive and that today I found him after all these years." Sean wiped the tears from his eyes.

"We usually turn a blind eye and leave him in peace. He's absolutely amazing for his age," commented the other policeman.

"He's a hero, my hero. He survived many bombing raids over Germany. He's been a great man," said Sean.

"It's so impressive, the story many of these old people have to tell," commented the other policeman to his colleague.

"OK, we didn't see you tonight," said one of the policemen, "but you need to take care of that father of yours. At his age he should be in aged care. This is a dangerous place at night and not the place for him."

"Oh, now that I've found him I intend to," replied Sean. "I totally agree that this is no place for someone his age."

The policemen left and Sean curled up and fell back into a deep sleep. It didn't seem that long afterwards that he felt a tapping on his shoulder. Sean slowly prised open his tired eyes again to find his father bending over him.

"We need to go if you want to make it back to your hotel before dawn."

Sean dragged himself up, still quite groggy. "Good I'll be able to take you out for a hearty breakfast, have a shower, then get you some new clothes and organise your flight back to New Zealand."

"I can't go, I don't have a passport," explained Danny. "Besides, I'm too old to go anywhere. I've lived my life."

"We'll just have to arrange a passport then," insisted Sean. "But meanwhile I can buy you a hearty breakfast and clothes."

"You can't get me a passport. If you remember I died in Sydney Harbour," added Danny.

"Oh! Well, there will surely be a way around it, Da," Sean insisted. "I can at least set you up in accommodation while I sort out the paperwork. Then I'll come back to America for you," reassured Sean. "I can't have my dad living like a tramp. We're not losing you again."

"But I'm happy here," replied Danny. "Anyhow we must leg it if you're to get back to your hotel before morning breaks."

Danny led the way through the Rambles to a shortcut where they could break through the bush to the road. Sean carried his gun under his jacket, preparing for the worst as the Rambles was not recommended as a safe walk in the dark. Along the track ahead they saw several people darting into the bushes. So it was true that Central Park had a number of residents. Sean, still half asleep, struggled to keep up with his father who was surprisingly fit.

"My eyes aren't too good these days so you're going to have to take the lead over the final stretch across that uneven ground through this jungle," said Danny, pointing ahead to a slightly trampled pathway leading off the track through vegetation. "We just go straight through there and the road is at the end."

"Well, one of the first things I'll have to do is buy you a Guinness," said Sean as he led the way, pushing carefully through the bush. "That's after we get good food into you, Da. Have to give it to you Da, you obviously know this park well." said Sean as he spotted the road and sidewalk ahead.

"Are you looking forward to a Guinness, Da?"

"Da?"

There was no reply. Sean looked behind him. His dad was not there.

"Da!" he yelled. But there was only silence and darkness in the bush behind him. Should he go back?

Sean hesitated, bursting into tears. Finally, he realised that his dad had chosen not to follow. Now he understood that his dad just wanted to spend his last remaining days living independently in a place he loved and called home. Had he understood earlier then he would have at least given his dad money to buy clothes and food. Maybe he could go back later in the day and find his dad. He decided that's what he'd do as he found the sidewalk. Sean placed the gun out of sight into his jacket pocket and continued on his way back to the hotel, catching a bus to soften the journey. Morning was now starting to break as he entered the hotel. The buffet was open and he felt extremely hungry, having not eaten for over 18 hours. He decided to have breakfast before returning to his room. That morning he had never eaten so much before and he still felt hungry as he left the breakfast room for the lobby and lift.

On entering the lobby for a minute he froze. A policeman with his back to him was talking to the receptionist. Sean briskly crossed the lobby, taking the stairway. The first thing I'm going to do is have a shower and get back into my own clothes, he thought.

Chapter Twenty-three

"History is an alternating series of frying pans and fires."

Peter Esterhazy

Sean turned the key in the door and entered his room. There, sitting at the table in his room, was a man reading his manuscript.

"Who are you and what are you doing in my room?" roared Sean, "and why are you dressed in my clothes? Get out."

The stranger at the table calmly raised his head and glared at Sean.

"Your room, you ignorant oaf? I paid for this room. This manuscript is rubbish!" he said in an Irish accent, throwing it back onto the table. "How can anyone, other than someone self-opinionated, seriously believe a publisher will host a writer, expenses all paid, for this type of rubbish?"

Sean stared at the man in disbelief. "What do you mean? Are you the publisher? Why, you look just like me! What's going on here?"

"Or is it that you look just like me?" teased the man. "Yes it all sounds very Irish. Are you so ignorant that you've never heard of the word doppelganger?"

"Doppelganger?" Sean repeated.

"You're supposedly the man with the literary knowledge. Do I have to explain it in plain English? You have a double, you oaf." The man paused before continuing. "We all have them, maybe three or four. Hitler, Churchill and others used them and I used you. I can assure you this isn't a mask, this is my real face."

"A double? I'm most certain we're not related." Sean looked flabbergasted.

"Thank goodness for that," taunted the man, a laugh escaping his mouth. "One has to admire Conor, a man of tenacity. When he realised we looked alike, he searched long and hard and finally found me, something Interpol has never succeeded in doing. And such a delightful proposition— too good for me to turn down. Bringing you to New York was a win-win for both of us."

"And how do I win?" asked Sean.

"Not you, you oaf, I'm talking about Conor. For me it made my task so much easier. The job is getting more and more difficult with electronic surveillance everywhere," replied the man.

"Who are you?" Sean asked. "Are you going to publish my book?"

"You wish! I'm the Mole Viper and you, my boy, have been my unsuspecting decoy and have done a great job. You see, while I've been planning on taking out two senators in Washington you've been parading around in my clothes drawing attention in New York. Conor was right and it has worked. I understand that there's been numerous sightings of the Mole Viper around New York."

"Now that explains everything, ever since I stepped foot into this country," replied Sean.

"What do you mean?" asked the Mole Viper.

"I'd hardly collected my bag before the airport security pounced on me. I was dragged away and interviewed by two Special Agents while customs officers checked baggage, shoes and everything. They even gave me a frisk search. They must have thought I was you. It did seem most odd at the time. Thank goodness that you insisted I bring a manuscript though. I was able to offer it as proof of being just a writer," explained Sean.

"And that was every good reason for me to enter over the Southern border, just like the cartel smugglers and terrorists," laughed the Mole Viper. "Conor did an amazing job keeping you moving around so you were seen but never bailed up by the police. While the police were more interested in finding me in New York I could go about my business in Washington."

"Well, he didn't do a great job yesterday when he had NYPD on my back thinking I was you," replied Sean. "He could have got me killed."

"That was the idea," laughed the man. "A good plan, but you're a little bit smarter than we thought. There was a time when it looked like this plan might never get off the ground."

"Oh?" murmured Sean.

"It just so happened that Conor looked like reneging after he first met you and discovered you weren't such a bad guy after all," said the Mole Viper.

"We were having a great time together," agreed Sean. "Touring around was fun."

"But," continued the Mole Viper, "once he realised you were callous and had no remorse and wouldn't want to change anything in your past if you could, he was, more than ever, keen for revenge. Obviously, you've made it back and Plan A has failed. But your timing today is impeccable."

"You were expecting me?" asked Sean.

"My boy, everything I do is meticulous. I don't just go out and shoot people. There's a lot of planning that goes into my operation and of course most essential is my exit plan and that's where Mohammed is most useful. Now we move to Plan B."

"Which is?" asked Sean.

"Oh, we have plenty of time and can get to that later." The Mole Viper placed a gun on the table. "You know that from this range I could put a hole through a dime if you were holding one."

Sean sat down on the edge of the bed and placed the jacket he was carrying in such a way that he could access his gun. He had been trained to use one by the IRA and at the time they thought he had shown promise.

"What surprises me," said Sean, "is that you're from the Middle East, yet your complexion is very European and you have an Irish accent."

"Ah, a very good point. My mother was Irish and my father was Persian. Yes, I have a very good Irish accent," explained the Mole Viper.

"Your mother was Irish?" asked Sean.

"Yes, in the days of the Shah of Iran when we attracted overseas tourists, my mother was on an overseas experience travelling through the Middle East when she met my dad. I grew up speaking both Persian and English which has been most helpful in my career."

"Not only do we share Irish ancestry," added the Mole Viper, "but you and I are very alike in many ways. Maybe somehow we are genetically related but that's no reason why I shouldn't shoot you."

"I don't think we're at all alike." Sean surreptitiously slipped his hand into the jacket pocket, sliding out the revolver and holding it under his jacket with his hand on the trigger. He had practiced many times as a youth shooting a slug gun from the same sitting position in the backyard.

"Well, I do," argued the Mole Viper. "You see, you're just as cold-blooded as me. I'll do what it takes to kill my target, even if it means killing others. I have no conscience and neither have you. You would walk into the Shankill Pub tomorrow, given the chance, but this time do a better job. You're a killer just like me and, like me, you're getting tired of having to watch your back all the time for people like Conor."

"I don't agree," replied Sean. "You kill for greed and are a coward whereas I'm a soldier and a hero."

"Soldier, what rubbish! I would have thought planting a bomb and just walking away was cowardly," he mocked. "So they killed your father and mother and oh dear, poor Colleen in Perth could be next. In fact I think she will. My pleasure."

"You leave Colleen out of it. She had nothing to do with the bombing," shouted Sean.

"She and her husband are not that innocent," laughed the Mole Viper. "And I believe that they're planning a bomb."

"What! How on earth do you know all these things?" Sean looked shocked.

"Yes, you know I think she will be next. Then there's little old Susie next door. You've never figured out if she is a spy or just a very nosey neighbour. Are you going to share these worries with Father Ted when he comes to pick you up at the airport?"

"What!" Sean looked astounded. "How do you know all this?"

"Worrying isn't it, to know that for a seven figure sum I could have saved the gang a lot of trouble and taken your whole family out when you set foot in Sydney," the Mole Viper laughed. "It would have saved you a life of misery. But Conor has been amazing finding a look-alike with a similar Irish accent, and best of all a recluse." The Mole Viper chuckled and started to play with his gun. "You know, I love guns and watching people drop as I squeeze the trigger."

"How do you know all these things about me?" Sean felt intimidated.

"I'm a professional and not a half-witted member of some gang. I carry out thorough research first," said the Mole Viper.

So these are your clothes that I'm wearing?" asked Sean.

"Correct, so you would look more like me as Conor paraded you around," he chuckled. "But you can keep them as I have your clothes now."

"Do you intend to shoot Conor since he knows a lot about you?" Sean probed.

"Oh, very devious. Ah, so you're looking for revenge?" The Mole Viper picked up his revolver and stared down the barrel. "No. I can only see one bullet there but it doesn't have Conor's name on it. No, I think I will let Conor live and maybe even give him Colleen's address in Perth." He chuckled again.

"At least I'm not a sadist," said Sean, realising his predicament, finger on the trigger and angling his position for a quick clean shot through the heart.

The Mole Viper stood there smugly, confident that he held all the cards and unaware of the weapon Sean was carrying.

"Well, in this situation your bomb-making knowledge is totally useless. Just a pity you were never trained in martial arts, knife throwing, guns or whatever. You do know that you're going to die today?" laughed the Mole Viper.

BANG!

One shot rang out and five minutes later the policeman who had been in the lobby burst through the door with his gun drawn.

"The Mole Viper," said the man standing over the prostrate lifeless body, a gun still in his hand.

"Drop the gun!" ordered the policeman.

"I'm Sean, an Irishman on holiday," he said, dropping the gun. "It was self-defence."

"The policeman nervously continued to point his gun and at the same time called for backup. "I've got the Mole Viper."

Within less than twenty minutes the room was swarming with NYPD policemen keen to share the glory, until two FBI Special Agents and a forensic team arrived and nearly all but the initial policeman and several others with guns drawn were ordered out of the hotel room. In the lobby, news crews assembled and jostled for position but were barred from taking the lift and stairway and eventually were removed from the hotel lobby.

"Get a statement from the officer first on the scene," ordered Special Agent John Dizon, the FBI officer who appeared to be in charge.

Special Agent Ford took the NYPD policeman aside and noted down his story and his initial observations when entering the crime scene.

"One bullet, straight through the heart," reported one of the forensic crew. "Wouldn't be dead for more than say… thirty minutes."

"That's quick work," praised Dizon.

"Open and shut case on how he died," replied one of the forensic crew. Another one of the crew was checking to confirm the place of death.

Dizon looked at the man who claimed to be Sean, then at the body lying on the floor. "Hm, a doppelganger."

"Sorry, Sir?" said Special Agent Ford.

"They're two people who look like identical twins but are most probably unrelated. We all have a double somewhere in the world." Dizon looked puzzled. "Now why would we have two people who look alike in a murder scene?"

"A conundrum," said Ford. "But which one is the Mole Viper?"

"He is," said the man claiming to be Sean. "I found him in my room when I returned this morning."

"He's certainly dressed like the Mole Viper," commented Ford.

"Yes, but before our first man was on the scene there was time for clothing to have been changed," said Dizon.

"And the Mole Viper's trademark is a bullet through the heart," commented Ford.

"A large number of our homicides are a bullet through the heart," reminded Dizon. "And it is point-blank range."

"Tell me," asked John Dizon, turning to the man claiming to be Sean. "Do you remember Special Agent Ford and me from anywhere?"

"Oh, are you referring to the airport interrogation?" replied the man claiming to be Sean. "It wasn't much fun having all my bags searched as well as a frisk search."

"Only Sean would know about the airport," said Ford.

"You would think so," replied Dizon.

"He's got to be Sean. Everything matches up." Ford looked convinced.

Dizon probed further. "It came to our attention that you served in the IRA. Is that where you learned to shoot?"

"That was a long time ago in Belfast when I was a boy," explained the man claiming to be Sean. "I don't have a criminal record and if you recall at the airport I showed my manuscript as proof of who I was. Believe me the man on the floor is the Mole Viper. I was set up. Look here." The man claiming to be Sean strode over to the table and immediately the policemen in the room had their fingers ready to squeeze their triggers.

He picked up the manuscript and passed it to Dizon.

"Hm, I've seen this one before." Dizon stopped and looked again at the homicide scene. "Now we have two guns, both loaded and one fired. We need to run a check that the bullet that killed was from the same gun and we need fingerprints from both guns. Now, how come you had a gun in your possession? You definitely didn't bring it into the country."

The man looked at him. "It's not my gun."

"Then whose is it?" asked Ford.

"It belongs to an Irishman by the name of Conor O'Mahony, probably going by a different name. He lured me into coming to New York on the pretence of publishing my novel but it turned out that they were using me to be a decoy for the Mole Viper," explained the man.

"What, here in the Big Apple?" Ford asked.

"Correct. While the Mole Viper was in Washington killing two senators. It's a long story. And it could easily be me lying dead now on that floor, only the Mole Viper didn't know about the gun under my jacket. It was self-defence."

"Where can we contact this Conor O'Mahony?" asked Ford.

"How would I know? He just turned up at the hotel every day to show me New York. What I can tell you is that he is probably going by a different surname. The receptionist in the hotel can probably confirm my description."

"This does all sound very complicated, and we'll need to interview you more down at headquarters," said Dizon, shaking his head. "Meanwhile, we need to carry out checks on blood types, dental records, DNA, and fingerprints as a final check."

"Right Boss," replied Ford.

"Will I go to prison, like it was self-defence, shoot or be shot?" asked the man claiming to be Sean.

"If John Doe proves to be the Mole Viper…"

"Which he is," interrupted the man claiming to be Sean.

"Then it will definitely be self-defence," said Dizon, and you'll be a hero and free to return to New Zealand, but you're not in the clear yet, not by any measure."

"I have a plane to catch in two days," said the man claiming to be Sean.

"You'll be lucky. Where to?" asked Ford.

"New Zealand."

Chapter Twenty-four

"Never be a prisoner of your past. It was just a lesson, not a life sentence."

Anonymous

The flight from Auckland to Christchurch took just over an hour. Sean left the aircraft and collected his baggage, making his way towards the exit.

"Sean, howya? You walked right past me," laughed Father Ted who approached and gave him a huge hug. "It's good to have you home."

"Didn't see you, Father. A sixteen hour flight from New York and a further hour from Auckland, I'm somewhat jet-lagged," replied Sean, yawning.

"Should be OK," said the priest, looking at his watch as he helped him and his bags to the car parking area. "I think we will make it without having to pay. So how was the Big Apple?" he asked.

"You got the first part, big, right," replied Sean, followed by another yawn. "All those policemen carrying guns were intimidating. Conor, who showed me around until the boss was ready, gave me very good advice…"

"Oh, and what was that, might I ask?" enquired the Father as he started the car.

"He said not to look at the policemen or they're likely to come over to question you," replied Sean.

"And did they?"

"Thank goodness they didn't," replied Sean.

"Well, I have to say that at times you do come across as furtive," teased the priest. "Thank goodness you remembered that they shoot first and ask questions later. Is Conor's Irish?"

"Correct, he migrated from Northern Ireland to America to escape all the troubles," replied Sean.

"America has, over the centuries, been a popular place for Irish people to settle," informed the Priest. "Especially during the Potato Famine of the nineteenth century."

"They're certainly well represented in America," laughed Sean. "The country must be in very good hands."

The priest laughed. "From memory there have been at least seven or eight presidents with Irish heritage, including Kennedy and Roosevelt. So, was the publisher happy with your novel?"

"Very happy," lied Sean.

"So when will it be in circulation?" probed the Father as he changed car lanes.

"Now that's more difficult to answer," replied Sean.

"Oh!" The priest looked surprised.

"Well, the publisher is very fussy and wants to use his own proof readers and editors, cover designer and so forth so it might take some time," lied Sean. How's it been here in Christchurch?"

"You've been missing some wonderful Summer days," replied Father Ted. We've had a week of nor'westers bringing hot dry weather and it's not surprising that we're now on a high fire warning. The Port Hills are brown and tinder dry."

"A change from New York weather," replied Sean.

"Paddy was asking about whether you'd made a decision about his sister coming from Ireland," continued the priest. "His sister wanted to take advantage of the cheap airfares currently on offer. They are your family, your cousins. You can't just keep shutting yourself away from others, fearing that somebody somewhere has a bullet with your name on it."

"I've been thinking about that a lot recently," replied Sean.

"Good," replied the Father. "I hoped that you'd give it some thought."

 "My time away was a good opportunity to reflect on my past in respect to my future," continued Sean. "So much has happened since the bombing and I'm not getting any younger."

"None of us are," nervously laughed the priest.

"America was an adventure," continued Sean, "but one I would not repeat. Call me a recluse but I enjoy my privacy and I have no intention of opening up old wounds. I do not want Paddy's sister or any other family member to visit. That's final. I've made up my mind, Father."

"Oh, and I thought America would bring about a positive change in your life." The priest turned the car down another street.

"It has, Father. I'm a changed man and it has helped me to see life more clearly," replied Sean. "I'm also considering moving house."

"Moving where?"

"That has yet to be decided," replied Sean. "But it will be somewhere quiet and safe where I can live out my life in privacy."

The priest parked his car out the front of Sean's house and opened the boot. "Since you've been away, that black van across the road hasn't appeared."

"Oh!" Sean looked surprised. "Though it's only been a week."

"True, but it's still a mystery. I know that Susie seems very happy that it's gone." The priest removed the bags from the boot. They carried the bags to the house and the priest boiled the jug for a cuppa.

"It's good to be home," Sean commented as they retreated to the lounge. He collapsed into an armchair and could have fallen asleep had the priest not been there.

"Nothing like falling back into the old routines," chuckled the priest as he raised his cup to drink more tea.

Sean placed his cup on the table and rose to greet a new-comer at the door.

"How can I help you, Sergeant?" asked Sean.

"Don't be silly. I haven't missed your humour one bit," laughed Sergeant, who had made space in her busy police schedule to welcome home her friend. "Well aren't you going to invite me in?"

"Of course," laughed Sean. "But I did get you going for a bit."

"Irish men!" joked Sergeant, walking through to the lounge and joining Father Ted. The priest rose to make her a cup of tea.

"Sean was telling me that he has decided not to invite his cousin from Ireland," informed the priest.

"Good for you. I'm glad you've finally come to your senses," replied Sergeant. "The trip to America was of some use though I still think somewhat risky, given your past. There are a lot of Irish people in America you know and maybe some you would not want to run into."

"We were just discussing that very point about America being a popular Irish haunt," said Father Ted. "Sean is also talking about selling up."

"And moving where?" asked Sergeant. "This has been a safe haven for you for many years, unlike Sydney and Auckland. Do you really want to risk somewhere where we can't offer you protection?"

"I'm still thinking about it," said Sean.

"Susie was asking after you," said Sergeant. "She's very keen to know about your new book."

"Don't you mean to know what I wrote about China?" smirked Sean.

"Paddy's keen to visit," said the Father.

"At this time I'd rather not have any other visitors," said Sean. "I've had too much happen recently."

"Oh dear," responded the Father, "and I thought you were enjoying reminiscing about old times."

"And he's right," said Sergeant. "All the trouble started when he met Paddy."

"It's all about reuniting families, that can't be bad," added the Father.

"I totally agree. Whānau is extremely important," agreed Sergeant. "But in this case, there could still be somebody out there wanting to kill Sean."

"I hope you don't mind," said Sean, finishing his tea. "I'm really quite jaded and would like to take myself away and have a kip."

"That's very understandable, Sean," replied Sergeant. "We're just going, aren't we, Ted?"

Chapter Twenty-five

Several weeks later.

"The mystery of love is greater than the mystery of death."
Oscar Wilde

"You're certainly a changed man after your trip to America but I've not yet decided if it is for the better." Father Ted handed Sean a cup of coffee. "To think that as a true Irishman you were raised on tea and now after just one week in the USA you're drinking coffee."

"Well, the Americans brought me to my senses," Sean laughed. "They showed their disapproval of the English in the Boston tea party and now so have I," replied Sean. "Besides I've taken a liking to it but still nothing beats a jar of the black stuff."

"Ha, King George the third did get rather greedy with his tax on tea," laughed the priest. "I dare say there would have been a few American Irishmen in that protest."

The priest paused as Sergeant and a stranger walked into the lounge. "How ya?" greeted Father Ted "Can I get you a cup of tea or coffee?"

"A nice strong brew of coffee will be fine, Sir," replied the tall stranger in an American accent.

"Tea as usual," replied Sergeant. "Didn't tea originate in Asia, Ted?"

"It did indeed," replied the priest, "and it was Samuel Bewley, an Irish businessman, and not the English who introduced it to Ireland, I'll have you know. I'll make you some tea." Father Ted left for the kitchen.

"Sean, this is John. You may remember him from your trip to America," said Sergeant.

Sean had already gingerly eyed up the stranger. He stood up and they shook hands. "Yes, I recognised him when he walked in and am most surprised he's followed me back to New Zealand."

"Yes, it must have been such a traumatic time for you, almost being the victim of that notorious hit man, the Mole Viper," said John "but thank goodness he's now gone for good. It's satisfying to think that he screwed up on his last mission and both US senators are fit and healthy and back at work."

"What hit man? What's all this? You said nothing about this to me," complained Sergeant.

"Nor me," Father Ted shouted from the kitchen. "First I knew of it and who's this Mole Viper?"

"Sorry, I was quite shaken at the time and for weeks was in a state of shock. It was very traumatic standing there with a revolver pointing at me and knowing that I was about to die." replied Sean. "I've spent most of my life in fear of some deranged Irishman seeking revenge but never expected this to happen."

"And you didn't tell us," said Sergeant. "I did warn you that no good would come from your trip."

"I thought it best to say nothing and just let it pass without troubling others," explained Sean.

"He's a brave man after what he went through," continued John. "Believe me, it must have been a most traumatic experience."

"Would you say enough to put him off drinking tea?" teased Father Ted from the kitchen. Both John and Sergeant laughed.

"Now I need to put your mind at rest, Sean. You'll be wondering why I'm here. America is very bureaucratic, needing every 'i' dotted and every 't' crossed. Simply put, the law is an ass and I have a pedantic boss who says I need more information concerning the hit man's two accomplices before we can arrest them. Together with your signature and the Sergeant here as a witness, that should be sufficient," replied John.

"Could you not have saved an airfare and requested all these details over the phone or Internet?" Sean asked, as he walked across and turned on the lounge lights.

"A pragmatic approach but unfortunately not one that works in the USA. Our laws require a signed report and a witness as evidence in order to arrest our suspects," replied John. "Sorry, an electronic signature is insufficient."

"So you have the suspects in custody?" asked Sean as he strolled over to close the lounge curtains. He paused for a second in front of the window. Something moving in the dark outside had caught his eye. Suddenly there was a loud bang as the window exploded.

"No! Sean! Oh, Sean!" Sergeant rushed over to the prostrate body lying on the floor.

"It's not Sean." John Dizon stood there, emotionless. "It's not who you think."

"Don't be so silly and insensitive, of course it is. I've known Sean for at least twenty years. Well, call an ambulance somebody." Sergeant stood there over the body, sobbing while she continued checking his vital signs. "How can you just stand there?"

"It's not Sean then?" queried Father Ted who had rushed from the kitchen to the prostrate body.

"Sean's double, what we call a doppelganger," explained John. "This is the Mole Viper, an International hit man wanted by Interpol for many murders and assassinations. He lured Sean to New York to use as his decoy so he could set about shooting two senators in Washington while they were out playing golf. But if that wasn't sinister enough, he had an even more devious plan to become Sean, using New Zealand as a safe haven for his retirement. Here he could comfortably live out the rest of his life off the millions earned from hit jobs."

"Oh, Sean is dead! How can you be so sure this is your hit man?" Sergeant wiped the tears from her eyes and didn't look convinced.

"I'm sorry to say that Sean really is dead. He was the last victim of the Mole Viper," replied John.

"Dead!" cried Sergeant, weeping again. "Oh Sean."

"I'm so sorry. Look, if you don't believe me then I suggest that you check over there by the window. It's just a hunch but you may find a loaded revolver hidden in a vase or something behind those drapes," suggested John. "Even if the Mole Viper felt safe living in New Zealand, he was too cunning not to have a back-up plan just in case."

"Are you kidding? There's a killer out there? How do I know I won't get shot as well?" Sergeant was somewhat reluctant.

"Your New Zealand Armed Offenders squad is out there and hopefully they've already apprehended the shooter," said John.

Sergeant nervously walked over to the drapes and looked behind them. "Oh! You're right." She fished a revolver out from a vase in the corner and was tempted to fire it at the dead body spread out over the floor, now realising that he had killed her friend. "How did you know?"

"That's why he walked over to close the curtains. Seeing me, he suspected the game was up," explained John. "But we had anticipated that he may try and shoot his way out," said John.

"It's a mystery how you were able to tell them apart if both men looked alike," commented Father Ted. "This certainly looks like Sean to me, though he was never quite the same when he returned from America. He went off more than just his cuppa."

"A very good point," replied the FBI agent. "I can tell you that it wasn't easy and at the time we got it wrong. All the evidence suggested that our dead body was the hit man."

"What evidence?" asked Sergeant.

"Well, firstly the dead man was dressed in the Mole Viper's clothes and the other was dressed as I remembered Sean when he entered the country."

"You had met him before?" Sergeant looked surprised.

"Well, we'd been tipped off that a man fitting the Mole Viper's description was flying into New York; that's why I was at the airport," explained John.

"Surely, you must have carried out fingerprint tests, looked at dental records, DNA tests or even the Iris Recognition tests used on passports," suggested Sergeant. "These days there are plenty of ways of identifying a dead body."

"Yes, I know but neither Sean nor the Mole Viper had criminal records, meaning no fingerprints nor DNA records to check against. Similarly, Sean's passport had no eye recognition and we had nothing to check against, not even dental records. Believe me, this was a conundrum," said John. "It wasn't as if we just put the shooting down to self-defence and let him leave the country. Believe me, we extensively interrogated him further at FBI headquarters but in the end all the circumstantial evidence pointed to him being Sean."

"Then what made you change your mind, may I ask?" The priest looked puzzled.

"Tell me, was Sean left or right handed?" asked John.

"Left handed, definitely," replied Sergeant.

"He was indeed," confirmed the Father.

"And when he shook my hand, which hand did he use?" asked John.

"Oh, I never thought about that. He shook with his right hand," said Sergeant. "Oh!"

"And to put it mildly, unlike a true Irishman, Sean was always reluctant to shake hands," added Father Ted, "but you did extend your hand first."

"And when he went to close the curtains, which hand did he use?"

"The right hand, I think," replied Sergeant, wiping her bloodshot eyes.

"When I interviewed Sean at the airport I suspected him to be the Mole Viper. At the time he reached into the contents from his case with his left hand to draw out his manuscript as proof," explained John.

"Was the manuscript sufficient to convince you he wasn't?" asked the Father.

"No, not at all," replied John. "A doppelganger never crossed my mind. This man, apart from his dress, had to be the Mole Viper. As I said before, we're not in the habit of letting people who meet the description of a terrorist just walk into our country. It was not until I spoke with a CIA agent who had been sitting next to him on the plane, that I learned that this was not the Mole Viper."

"Sean was of interest to the CIA?" A tearful Sergeant looked surprised.

"Oh yes," replied John.

"At the time when I entered the murder scene I was faced with a conundrum: two identical men: one claiming to be Sean and to have shot in self-defence and the other who was dead but which one was which? Of course the one who is alive will naturally claim they're not the Mole Viper. The other day I was reading the report by the first policeman on the scene and it was then I realised we had made a terrible mistake, that the Mole Viper had once again eluded the FBI and Interpol."

"What was that?" Sergeant wiped the tears from her eyes.

"The policeman who entered the hotel room first found the gun in the right hand of the shooter," said John.

"Ah, that does all now make sense," replied Sergeant. "And he never seemed the same after returning from America. Even Susie, next door, commented to that effect."

"And a true Irishman never gives up his tea for coffee," added Father Ted.

"How did Sean die?" sobbed Sergeant.

"It would have been fast, Sergeant. Just one bullet through the heart. It would have been quick and painless," replied John, showing more empathy. "Like the Mole Viper, a snake, he came from the Middle East and killed with a shot to the heart. This hit man and his loyal associate were both marksmen and most times did a clean job. I think that it's time we had that coffee, Father" said John, taking a seat.

"Oh! Poor, poor Sean," cried Sergeant, as the tears rolled out of her eyes. "Here he was scared of dying at the hands of some Irish psychopath but was lured to his death in America for a totally different reason?"

"It seems that way," replied John. "Though there still seems to be missing pieces to this puzzle."

"What missing pieces?" asked Sergeant.

"John?" said a man in plain clothes coming into the room.

"Oh, this is Special Agent Jones," said John. "This is Sergeant…ah, and Father…ah…"

"You had this place staked out and didn't tell me?" Sergeant looked angrily at John.

"Sorry, we needed you to approach the subject, hopefully without raising suspicion. He was a very dangerous character and sorry, but we were operating over your head with your boss's approval."

"John, we managed to apprehend the shooters." Jones looked very pleased.

"Oh, good," replied John.

"One was taken out by the New Zealand first offender's squad and the John Doe is Mohammed Abadi," informed Jones.

"Mohammed, well done, that's his right-hand man," said John. "Now why would he take out his own boss who he was very fond of and loyal to?"

"Maybe he too was fooled and believed it was Sean he was shooting," suggested Sergeant.

"Yes, of course, that could be it. He wouldn't have been expecting his boss to desert him and to retire without telling him." said John. "With Interpol believing he was dead, he couldn't afford to tell anyone, not even Mohammed."

"And that would appear to be the case," replied Jones. "The driver was a guy called Conor, an Irishman. He swears he couldn't even kill a spider; that Mohammed did the shooting."

"An Irish man!" the priest looked surprised.

"I believe him," replied John. "Mohammed, just like the Mole Viper, was a cold-blooded killer and would have insisted on pulling the trigger in seeking revenge. Mohammed was also an excellent marksman."

"Conor said that they were both convinced Sean had killed the Mole Viper. He's pleased to see the end of Sean and his father for destroying their lives."

"Ah, so in the end an Irish connection to Sean's murder," commented Sergeant. "I was right, after all these years there was at least one Irishman still seeking revenge."

Sergeant wiped her eyes. The shock of Sean being dead was unsettling. They had become very close over many years and she would miss him immensely.

"The other thing that convinced me that we'd let the wrong man go was a message I received from the CIA," added John. "Sean had been under surveillance. An operative very close to Sean had commented that the man who'd returned from the USA seemed different," said John.

"Who was the operative?" asked Sergeant.

"You know he can't tell you that even if he did know," said Father Ted.

"It must be Susie," said Sergeant. "Who else apart from us was close to Sean?"

"Now you leave poor Susie out of it," teased Father Ted. "She's just a little harmless old woman."

Father Ted looked sympathetically towards Sergeant. "I'm so sorry for you, Sergeant. Revenge is such a terrible, terrible thing. Sean lost his parents, you've lost a friend and Conor's lost his freedom. There are no winners, only victims in a cycle of hatred and revenge. If only people could learn to forgive and to move on with life. Next to loving God, Jesus said that the second most important thing in life is to love our neighbour."

"But who is our neighbour?" asked Sergeant.

"May the road rise up to meet you.

May the wind be always at your back.

May the sun shine warm upon your face;

the rains fall soft upon your fields

and until we meet again,

may God hold you in the palm of His hand."

Amen

(An ancient Celtic prayer)

As a friend and former workmate, I have known Brian for over thirty years. We have shared some of the same interests such as tramping in the New Zealand Southern Alps and a passion for serving our workmates as workplace delegates.

Brian has accounting and management qualifications and an MA(honours) in psychology and has used this knowledge to good advantage in his work and personal life.

After Brian retired, I expected him to do the usual things such as lawn bowling and gardening. I never expected him to write books. Brian's first four books were well written short stories using his experiences in life such as the Christchurch earthquakes, mountain adventures and overseas travel through the Pacific, Europe and Asia. Brian has now also written four novels and with ten grandchildren has also found time to write three children's books.
I am very impressed with how his writing style has developed in these novels.

Andrew Thirring

Dear Reader,

I hope you enjoyed this novel

Please consider leaving a review on the
Internet

Bookselling sites

Thank you

186